"Do You Remember Asking Me If Italians Make New Year's Resolutions?"

His face cast in shadows, Marco reached up to tuck a wayward strand behind Sabrina's ear.

"I do. And as I recall, you said that was an all-American tradition."

"I've decided to make one tonight."

She had to smile at his solemn expression. "Want to tell me what it is?"

"It's you, Sabrina *mia.*"

As if consumed by the need to touch her, Marco drew his fingertips across her cheek, brushed her lips, cupped her chin. "I know we agreed to move one step at a time. I know I'm pushing when I should be patient. But I've resolved to do whatever I can, whatever I must, to keep you in Italy. And in my heart."

Sheer surprise took her breath away.

Dear Reader,

Did you ever stumble on a place that just took your breath away? My husband and I did when we drove down from Rome and meandered along Italy's Amalfi Coast with two of our best friends. I'll never forget my first view of Positano, with its colorful villas stair-stepping down a steep hillside to the achingly blue Mediterranean Sea. Like the heroine of this book, I was completely blown away.

I knew I had to write a story set in that fascinating locale someday, and when I started plotting the HOLIDAYS ABROAD series, the Amalfi Coast leapt instantly to mind. So sit back, sip a glass of limoncello if you can find it, and celebrate the New Year with a hunky duke in one of the most glorious spots on earth.

All my best,

Merline Lovelace

MERLINE LOVELACE

THE DUKE'S NEW YEAR'S RESOLUTION

Published by Silhouette Books
America's Publisher of Contemporary Romance

Recycling programs for this product may not exist in your area.

ISBN-13: 978-0-373-76913-1
ISBN-10: 0-373-76913-X

THE DUKE'S NEW YEAR'S RESOLUTION

This edition published by arrangement with Harlequin Books S.A.

Visit Silhouette Books at www.eHarlequin.com

Printed in U.S.A.

Books by Merline Lovelace

Silhouette Desire

†*Devlin and the Deep Blue Sea* #1726
**The CEO's Christmas Proposition* #1905
**The Duke's New Year's Resolution* #1913

Silhouette Romantic Suspense

†*Diamonds Can Be Deadly* #1411
†*Closer Encounters* #1439
†*Stranded with a Spy* #1483
†*Match Play* #1500
†*Undercover Wife* #1531

Silhouette Nocturne

Mind Games #33

†Code Name: Danger
**Holidays Abroad

MERLINE LOVELACE

A retired Air Force officer, Merline Lovelace served at bases all over the world, including tours in Taiwan, Vietnam and at the Pentagon. When she hung up her uniform for the last time, she decided to combine her love of adventure with her flair for storytelling, basing many of her tales on her experiences in the service.

Since then, she's produced more than seventy-five action-packed novels, many of which have made the *USA TODAY* and Waldenbooks bestseller lists. Over nine million copies of her works are in print in thirty-one countries. Named Oklahoma's Writer of the Year and the Oklahoma Female Veteran of the Year, Merline is also a recipient of Romance Writers of America's prestigious RITA® Award.

When she's not glued to her keyboard, she and her husband enjoy traveling and chasing little white balls around the fairways of Oklahoma. Check her Web site at www.merlinelovelace.com for news, contests and information about upcoming releases.

Be sure to watch for the third book in the Holidays Abroad series, *The Executive's Valentine Seduction,* coming next month from Silhouette Desire.

To our traveling buds, Sue & Pat,
who shared the glories of the Amalfi Coast with us
despite the knuckle-biting roads and one sprained ankle.
Next stop—the Pyramids! And very special thanks to
Elizabeth Jennings, doyen of Italy's fabulous
Women's Fiction Festival and the kind, patient
fellow author who straightened out my mangled Italian.

One

Sabrina Russo got only a few seconds' warning before disaster struck.

The powerful roar of a vehicle rounding the hairpin curve behind her carried clearly on the late December air. Cursing, she kicked herself for parking her rental car in a turnout a good ten yards back. The roads on this portion of Italy's Amalfi coast were narrow and treacherous at best. Walls of sheer rock hedged the pavement on one side, thousand-foot drops on the other. But, like the worst kind of numbnuts tourist, she'd *had* to leave the protection of the turnout and inch along this narrow, pebble-strewn verge to snap a picture of the colorful village spilling down the steep mountainside to the blue-green Mediterranean below.

The slick leather soles of her boots provided only marginal traction as she scrambled back toward the turnout. She was still trying to reach its protective guardrail when a flame-red Ferrari convertible swept around the curve.

Sabrina caught a glimpse of the driver—just a glimpse. Her frantic mind registered dark hair, wide shoulders encased in a buckskin-tan-colored jacket, and a startled expression on a face so strong and chiseled it might have been sculpted by Michelangelo. Then the Ferrari was aiming right for her.

"Hey!"

Yelping, she leaped back. She knew she was in trouble when her left boot heel came down on empty air. Faced with the choice of throwing herself forward, under the Ferrari's tires, or toppling down the steep precipice behind her, she opted for the tumble.

She didn't fall far, but she hit hard. The cell phone she'd been using to shoot the photos flew out of her hands. A rocky outcropping slammed into her hip. Her gray wool slacks and matching, hip-length jacket protected her from the stony, serrated edges. The wool provided little buffer, however, when she crashed into a stunted, wind-tortured tree that clung to the cliffside with stubborn tenacity.

Pain shot from her ankle to her hip in white-hot waves. The achingly blue Mediterranean sky blurred around the edges.

* * *

"Signorina! Signorina! Mi sente?"

A deep, compelling voice pierced the gray haze. Sabrina fought the agony shooting through her and turned her head.

"Ecco, brava. Apra gli' occhi."

Slowly, so slowly, a face swam into view.

"Wh—what happened?"

"Siete..." He gave a quick shake of his head and shifted to flawless English. "You fell from the road above. Luckily, this cypress broke your descent."

Sabrina blinked, and a twisted tree trunk came into focus. Its thin branches and silvery-green leaves formed a backdrop for the face hovering over her. Even dazed and confused, she felt its sensual impact.

The man was certifiably gorgeous! Whiskers darkened his cheeks and strong, square chin. His mouth could tempt a saint to sin, and Sabrina was certainly no candidate for canonization. His short, black hair had just a hint of curl, and his skin was tanned to warm oak.

But it was his eyes that mesmerized her. Dark and compelling, they stared into hers. For an absurd moment, she had the ridiculous notion he was looking into her soul.

Then more of her haze cleared and she recognized the driver of the Ferrari. Anger spiked through her, overriding the pain.

"You almost hit me!"

She planted a hand against the tree trunk and

tried to sit up. The attempt produced two immediate reactions. The first was a searing jolt that lanced from her ankle to her hip. The second was a big hand splayed against her shoulder, accompanied by a sharp order.

"Be still! You're not bleeding from any external wounds, but you may have sustained a concussion or internal injuries. Tell me, do you hurt when you breathe?"

She drew in a cautious breath. "No."

"Can you move your head?"

She tried a tentative tilt. "Yes."

"Lie still while I check for broken bones."

"Hey! Watch where you put those hands, pal!"

Impatience stamped across his classic features. "I am a doctor."

Good excuse to cop a feel, Sabrina thought, too pissed to appreciate his gentle touch.

"You have no business taking these hairpin turns so fast," she informed him. "Especially when there's no guardrail. I had nowhere to go but down. If I hadn't hit this tree I could have… Ow!"

She clenched her teeth against the agony when he ran his hands down her calf to her ankle.

Frowning, the doc sat back on his heels. "With your boot on, I can't tell if the ankle is broken or merely sprained. We must get you to the hospital for X-rays."

He glanced from her to the road above and back again.

"My cell phone is in the car. I can call an ambulance. Unfortunately, the closest will have to come from the town of Amalfi, thirty kilometers from here."

Terrific! Thirty kilometers of narrow, winding roads with blind curves and snaking switchbacks. She'd be down here all day, clinging to this friggin' tree.

"It's better if we get you to the car and I drive you to the hospital myself."

Sabrina eyed the slope doubtfully. "I don't think I'm up for a climb."

"I'll carry you."

He said it with such self-assurance that she almost believed he could. He had the shoulders for it. They looked wide and solid under his suede bomber jacket.

Sabrina was no lightweight, however. She kept in shape with daily workouts, but her five-eight height and lush curves added up to more pounds than she cared to admit in polite company.

"Thanks, anyway, but I'll wait for the ambulance."

"You could black out again or go into shock." Pushing to his feet, he braced himself at an angle on the slope and issued a brusque order. "Take my hand."

The imperious command rubbed her exactly the wrong way. She'd spent a turbulent childhood and her even more tempestuous college years rebelling against her cold, autocratic father. She'd paid the price for her revolt many times over, but she still didn't take orders well.

"Anyone ever tell you that you need to work on your bedside manner, Doc? It pretty well sucks."

His dark brows snapped together in a way that clearly said he wasn't used to being taken to task by his patients. She answered with a bland smile. After a short staring contest, his scowl relaxed into a reluctant grin.

"I believe that has been mentioned to me before."

The air left Sabrina's lungs a second time. The man was seriously hot without that crooked grin. With it, he made breathing a lost cause.

"Shall we start again?" he suggested in a less impatient tone. "I am Marco Calvetti. And you are?"

"Sabrina Russo."

"Allow me to help you up to the car." He reached down a hand. "If you please, Signorina Russo."

It was either wait for the ambulance or take him up on his offer. No choice, really. Sabrina needed to get her ankle looked at and be on her way. She had business to take care of. Important business that could put the fledgling company she'd started with her two best friends into the black for the first time since they'd launched it.

She laid her hand in his, her nerves jumping when his fingers folded around hers. Loose stones rattled and skittered down the slope as she levered up and onto her uninjured leg. Once vertical, she got a good look at the sheer precipice only a few yards beyond her tree.

"Oh, God!"

"Don't look down. Put your arm around my neck."

When she complied, he lifted her and hooked an elbow under her knees. She could feel the muscles go taut under the buttery suede as he made his careful way up the slope. Determined not to look down, she kept her gaze locked on his profile.

The dark bristles sprouting on his cheeks and chin only accentuated his rugged good looks. He had a Roman nose, she decided, straight and strong and proud. His eyes were a clear, liquid brown. And was that a sprinkling of silver at his temple?

Interesting man. When he wasn't trying to run people down, that is. The black skid marks leading to the convertible nosed onto the narrow verge made Sabrina bristle again.

"You came around that corner way too fast. If I hadn't jumped backward, you would have hit me."

"You should not have left the safety of the turnout," he countered. "Why did you do something so foolish?"

She hated to admit she'd been mesmerized by the incredible view and was snapping pictures like an awestruck tourist, but she had no other excuse short of an outright lie. Sabrina had committed more than her share of sins in her colorful past. Lying wasn't one of them.

"I was taking pictures. For my business," she added, as if that would lessen the idiocy.

He didn't roll his eyes but he came damned close. "What business is that?"

"My company provides travel, translation and executive support services for Americans doing business in Europe. I'm here to scout locations for a high-level conference for one of our clients."

He nodded, but made no comment as they approached the red convertible. Raising a knee, he balanced her on a hard, muscled thigh and reached down to open the passenger door. Despite her efforts to protect her ankle, Sabrina was gritting her teeth by the time he'd jockeyed her into the seat.

"My purse," she ground out. "It's in the rental car."

He did the almost-eye-roll thing again.

Okay, so leaving her purse unattended in Italy—or anywhere else!—wasn't the smartest thing to do. She certainly wouldn't have done so under normal circumstances. But this was such an isolated stretch of road and she'd kept her rental car in view the whole time. Except when she'd nose-dived over the side of the cliff, of course.

Good thing she *didn't* have her purse with her then. If she had, it might have gone the way of her cell phone. God knew where that was right now. One thing's for sure, she wasn't crawling back down the slope to look for it.

"I locked your car," the doc informed her when he returned with her purse and the keys. "I'll send someone back for it while you're being attended to."

He folded his muscular frame behind the wheel with practiced ease and keyed the Ferrari's ignition. It came to life with a well-mannered growl.

"I'll take you to the clinic in Positano. It's small but well equipped."

"How far is that?"

"Just there." He indicated the cluster of colorful buildings clinging to the side of the cliff. "The place you were photographing," he added on a dry note.

Sabrina was too preoccupied at the moment to respond. Navigating these narrow, twisting roads in the driver's seat was nerve-racking enough. Sitting in the passenger seat, with a perpendicular drop-off mere inches away, it was a life-altering experience.

Stiff-armed, she braced her palms against the edge of her seat. Her uninjured leg instinctively thumped the floorboards, searching for the nonexistent brake on every turn. She sucked air whenever the Ferrari took a curve but gradually, grudgingly, had to admit the doc handled his powerful machine with unerring skill. Which didn't explain why he'd seemed to aim right for her a while ago.

She must have startled him as much as he had her. Obviously, he hadn't expected to encounter a pedestrian on that narrow curve. He wouldn't encounter this one again, Sabrina vowed as the convertible hugged the asphalt on another switchback turn. She'd learned her lesson. No more excursions beyond the protection of the guardrails.

Dragging her attention from the sheer precipices, she pinned it on the driver. "Your name and accent are Italian, but your English has a touch of New York City in it."

"You have a good ear. I did a three-year neurosurgical residency at Mount Sinai. I still consult there and fly over two or three times a year." He sent a swift glance in her direction. "Are you a New Yorker?"

"I was once," she got out, her uninjured foot stomping the floorboard again. "How about you keep your eyes on the road, Doc?"

She didn't draw a full breath until the road cut away from the cliffs and buildings began to spring up on her side of the car.

Positano turned out to be a small town but one that obviously catered to the tourist trade during the regular season. This late in the year, many of the shops and restaurants were shuttered. Those still open displayed windows filled with glazed pottery and bottles of the region's famous limoncello liqueur.

The town's main street led straight down to a round-domed church and a piazza overlooking the sea, then straight up again. Since it was only two days past Christmas, the piazza was still decorated with festive garlands. A life-size nativity scene held the place of honor outside the church. Sabrina caught a glimpse of colorful fishing boats pulled up on a slice of rocky beach just before the doc made a sharp left and pulled into a small courtyard.

Killing the engine, he came around to the passenger side of the Ferrari. Once again she looped her arm around his neck. Her cheek brushed his when he lifted her. The bristles set the nerves just under her skin to dancing as he carried her toward a set of double glass doors.

The doors swished open at their approach. The nurse at the counter glanced up, her eyes widening in surprise.

"Sua Eccellenza!"

Sabrina's German and French were much better than her Italian, but she was fairly certain nurses didn't routinely accord physicians the title of Your Excellency. The rest of their conversation was so machine-gun fast, however, she didn't have time to figure that one out before the nurse rushed forward with a wheelchair.

"Rafaela will take you to X-ray," the doc said as he lowered her into the chair. "I'll speak with you after I review the films."

She must look like she'd just fallen off a cliff, Sabrina thought ruefully. The nurse gave her a fish-eyed stare until a sharp order from the doc put her in motion. With a squeak of the chair's rubber wheels, she propelled Sabrina through another set of double doors.

Marco remained in the reception area for a long time after the doors swished shut. He couldn't blame Rafaela for gaping at this woman, this Sabrina Russo. The resemblance was incredible.

So incredible, he'd almost lost control of his car when he'd spotted her back there on that narrow road. Thank the Lord instinct had taken over from his shocked brain! Without thinking, he'd cut back into the proper lane and jammed on the brakes.

Then his only concern was getting to her, making sure she'd survived the fall. But now…

Now there was nothing to keep him reliving those terrifying seconds just before she fell. One thought and one thought only hammered into his skull.

He might have killed her. Again.

His jaw clenched so tight his back teeth ground together. Unseeing, Marco stared at the double doors. A phone buzzed somewhere in the distance. Outside, a horn honked with typical Italian impatience.

He heard nothing, saw nothing but the image of the woman who'd disappeared behind the doors. Her face, her features remained vivid in his mind as he reached into the inside pocket of his jacket.

The picture he drew out of his wallet was old and dog-eared. It was the only snapshot he hadn't been able to bring himself to pack away. His throat tight, he stared down at the laughing couple.

He'd been in his early twenties, a premed student at the University of Milan. Gianetta was three years younger. She looked so vibrant, so alive in this faded picture that a fist seemed to reach into Marco's chest and rip out his beating, bleeding heart.

How young they'd been then. How blinded by lust. So sure their passion would stand the test of time. So heedless of the words of caution both his family and hers felt compelled to voice.

He should have listened, Marco thought savagely. He'd been premed, for God's sake! He should have recognized the signs. The soaring highs. The sudden lows. The wild exuberance he'd ascribed to the mindless energy of youth. The seeds had been there, though. He could see them now in the laughing face turned up to the camera.

A face that was almost the mirror image of Sabrina Russo's.

She could be Gianetta's sister. Her twin. They had the same sun-streaked blond hair. The same slanting brown eyes. The same stubborn chin.

Or…

His stomach knotting, Marco echoed the irrational, improbable thought that had leaped into his mind when he'd glimpsed the woman in the road.

She could be his wife.

Gianetta, who had insisted on launching the sailboat despite the weather warnings.

Gianetta, whose frantic radio call for help still haunted his dreams.

Gianetta, whose body had never been recovered from the sea.

With a muttered oath, Marco shook his head. He'd been working too hard. Performing too many difficult surgeries. The long hours and unrelenting pace had gotten to him. How absurd to fantasize for so much as a single second that this American, this Sabrina Russo, could be his dead wife!

He was glad now his surgical team had pleaded

with him to take a long-overdue break between Christmas and New Year's. Obviously, he needed it.

With another impatient shake of his head, he pushed through the double doors and strode down the hall toward X-ray.

Two

Wincing, Sabina swung her legs off the X-ray table and sat up on the edge. The remains of the boot they'd had to cut off lay discarded beside the table.

"Allow me to assist you, Ms. Russo."

Rafaela nudged the wheelchair closer. After a somewhat graceless transfer, the nurse got Sabrina settled into the chair.

"I shall take you to an exam room, yes? Dr. Calvetti will review the X-rays and consult with you there."

"You called him something else when we first came in," Sabrina commented as she was wheeled into the corridor. "*Eccellenza,* wasn't it?"

"Si."

"What's with that?"

"He prefers to use his medical title here at the clinic, but I forget myself sometimes. My mother cooks and cleans for him when he's in residence at his villa, you see."

"Not really. Who is he?"

"His Excellency Don Marco Antonio Sonestra di Calvetti, twelfth Duke of San Giovanti, fourteenth Marquis of Caprielle, ninth Marquis d'Almalfi, Count Palatine, sixteenth Baron of Ravenna..." She paused. "Or is it the seventeenth Baron Ravenna?"

"You got me."

"There are more titles. Many more." Smiling, Rafaela steered her patient into an exam room and set the brake. "Mama can recite the entire list without taking a breath. She has worked for the Calvetti family since she was a young girl."

Okay, Sabrina was impressed. So the doc was also a duke. Not to mention a world-class hunk. The combination was almost enough to make her forget how close His Excellency had come to flattening her into roadkill.

But not quite enough to keep her from scowling when he delivered the good news/bad news.

"The X-rays show no sign of concussion or fractured bones in your ankle. However, you may have damaged or torn a ligament. We won't know for sure until we perform a stress test."

"Where and when do we do that?"

"It's a simple test. A manipulation of the foot and ankle. I'll do it now if you can stand the pain."

Uh-oh! That didn't sound good.

"Once we are done, I will prescribe painkillers. But you must be alert for the manipulation, so you can tell me when I hurt you."

When, not if. That sounded even worse.

"Okay, Doc, let's get this over with. Or should I say duke?"

"Either will suffice." Those dark eyes held hers. "Given the circumstances, perhaps we should dispense with titles altogether."

She wasn't sure exactly what circumstances he referred to but had no problem with a more egalitarian approach. "That's fine with me."

"Good. You must call me Marco. And may I call you Sabrina?"

She granted the polite request with a regal nod. "You may."

"Very well, Sabrina. Rafaela and I will help you onto the exam table."

She managed it with their assistance and a couple of hops. Once they had her in place, Rafaela rolled up the hem of the wool slacks. The bruised, inflated sausage she revealed made Sabrina grimace.

"Lovely," she muttered.

"It will get worse before it gets better," the doc—duke—Marco warned.

He washed his hands at the sink in the exam room. The scent of antibacterial soap came with him as he rolled a stool close to the table, seated himself and cupped her heel. His touch was gentle, lulling Sabrina into a false sense of security. That lasted only until he flattened his other hand against her shin and applied pressure. The pain almost brought her off the table.

"Okay, okay," she gasped. "You found the not-so-sweet spot."

He relieved the frontal pressure and applied it sideways. More prepared this time, Sabrina merely gritted her teeth.

"It is not as bad as I feared," he said when he'd completed the test.

"Easy for you to say!"

"I don't believe you've torn the ligaments, merely strained them. We will wrap the ankle in a compression bandage. Then you must stay off your feet, apply ice and take the painkillers I will prescribe."

"Stay off my feet for how long?"

"As a minimum, until the swelling goes down and the pain lessens. After that, you may require crutches for a few days to a week."

"A week!"

Sabrina swallowed a groan. Her tight schedule was disintegrating before her eyes. She'd already rearranged it once to spend Christmas Day in Austria with her two best friends and business partners.

Sabrina, Devon McShay and Caroline Walters had met years ago while spending their junior year studying at the University of Salzburg. Filled with the dreams and enthusiasm of youth, the three coeds had formed a fast friendship. They'd maintained that friendship long distance in the years that followed. Until last May, when they'd met for a minireunion.

After acknowledging that their lives hadn't lived up to their dreams, they'd decided to pool resources. Two months later, they'd quit their respective jobs and launched European Business Services, Incorporated. EBS for short. Specializing in arranging transportation, hotels, conference facilities, translation and other support services for busy executives.

Now Devon McShay, the former history professor, Caroline Walters, the quiet, introverted librarian, and Sabrina the one-time rebel and good-time girl were hard-nosed businesswomen. They had an office and a small staff in a Washington, D.C., suburb and had spent megabucks on advertising. They'd landed a few jobs, but nothing big until aerospace mogul Cal Logan hired EBS to work his short-notice trip to Germany.

Sabrina had done most of the frantic prep work for Logan's five-day, three-city blitz, but came down with the flu the day before she was supposed to fly to Germany. Devon took the trip instead, with some interesting results. Sexy Cal Logan had made it plain he wanted to merge more than business interests with Devon.

Dev was now scrambling to put together a conference for high-level Logan Aerospace executives while Caroline and Sabrina divided forces to scout locations for the lucrative new contract they'd just landed with Global Security International.

Their client wanted to hold the conference the second week in February in either Italy or Spain. Caro and Sabrina had jumped on the computer to find locations with sufficient available rooms and conference facilities on such short notice.

Their choices narrowed to a handful of potential sites, Caro flew into Barcelona to physically inspect those along Spain's Costa Bravo. Sabrina was supposed to check the possibilities here, on Italy's Amalfi Coast. They had less than two weeks to put together an acceptable proposal, and Sabrina wasn't about to let a little thing like a sprained ankle deter her.

There was another side to her determination. One that went deeper and struck at what she was. Or what she used to be. She'd struggled too long to get out of her father's shadow…and taken too much crap from him and his lawyers when she'd resigned from the board of the Russo Foundation to go into business with her two friends. Sabrina fully intended to make it on her own *and* make a success of EBS, which meant hopping off this exam table and getting her butt in gear.

She aimed her best smile at the doc/duke. "Bring on the ace bandage and painkillers, and I'll be on my way."

"Your way to where?"

"I'm booked in a hotel in Ravello tonight. I'm scouting it as a possible conference site."

According to Sabrina's research, the picturesque

mountaintop resort was only a short distance from Positano as the crow flew. Too bad she couldn't sprout wings. The trip would take forever on these tortuous roads.

"You cannot drive to Ravello if you take prescription narcotics," the doc countered firmly. "Or anywhere else, for that matter. Under Italian law you cannot drive at all."

"Great!" She blew out a frustrated breath. "Okay, forget the drugs. Just bandage me up, throw in a set of crutches and I'll gimp on down the coast."

Marco hesitated. He was tempted to comply with her request—extremely tempted. The woman's resemblance to Gianetta had shaken him more than he cared to admit. He would like nothing more than to send Sabrina Russo on her way and slam the door on the memories she'd stirred.

Unfortunately, his personal preferences conflicted with the oath he'd taken as a physician and the knowledge that he was at least partially responsibility for this woman's injury.

"I'm afraid you don't appreciate the seriousness of your sprain," he told his reluctant patient. "It will heal itself in time if you're careful. If you bring the wrong pressure to bear on your ankle, however, you could cause more serious damage that might require surgery to repair. Or leave you with a permanent limp."

She paled a little at that. Satisfied that he had her attention, Marco pressed on.

"I should like you to remain in Positano tonight.

I'll tend to your ankle and, if your condition allows, you may continue your journey tomorrow."

She gave in grudgingly. "I guess I have no choice."

"Very well. Rafaela, a pressure bandage, please."

The nurse had anticipated the request and had a rolled bandage in hand. She was every bit as efficient as her mama, Marco thought, pleased all over again that he'd paid her tuition to nursing school.

When he moved his stool closer and propped Sabrina's foot on his knee, her breath hissed in. Marco used his gentlest touch to wrap the ankle. The skin around the injured joint was distended, the bruising already vicious.

The calf above, however, was long and smooth and shapely. As he cupped the firm flesh, a jolt went through him. This time the shock had nothing to do with seeing what appeared to be the ghost of his dead wife. This time it was lust, hard and fast and hot.

Gesù! What possessed him today? Disgusted with himself, he caught only the tail end of his patient's question to Rafaela.

"...recommend a good hotel?"

"The tourist season is over, Signorina Russo. We have only one hotel still open. The five-star Le Sireneuse. It's quite elegant and very popular with film stars and visiting dignitaries. Their rooms are usually booked a year or more in advance, but I'll call and see if they have anything available, yes?"

"Thanks."

Rafaela slid out the cell phone clipped to her waist and made the quick call.

"It's as I feared, Signorina. The hotel is fully booked. I'll try The Neptune. It's just outside town and may still be open."

Marco brought the bandage under a delicate arch and waged a fierce internal debate. His gut told him to say nothing, to let this woman find her own accommodations. She disturbed him in too many ways. Yet the sense of responsibility bred into him with his name and title would not allow him to ignore the fact he had contributed to her present predicament. Then there was that haunting resemblance to Gianetta…

"There's no need to call another hotel. You must stay at my villa tonight."

"Thanks, but I wouldn't want to impose."

"It is no imposition, I assure you. The villa is small, merely a vacation home, but has several guest suites. I should prefer to keep a watch on you to make sure you don't suffer any residual effects from the accident. And," he added with a smile for the nurse, "Rafaela's mama will cook for us. Rafaela will tell you her mama serves the best grilled swordfish on the Amalfi coast."

"It's true, Signorina. Mama's *pesce spada* will make you weep with joy." The young nurse kissed her fingertips in tribute to her mother's skills. "You will taste nothing like it."

"Well…"

"Good," Marco said. "It is settled. How does the bandage feel? Not too tight?"

His patient tried a tentative wiggle. "It's fine."

After securing the bandage with a Velcro strap, he carefully lowered her foot and rose. "Before I give you something for the pain, please tell me if you have ever experienced an adverse reaction to drugs or have a medical condition I should be aware of."

"No to both."

Marco considered the range of drugs available at the small clinic and wrote an order for an opiate that would provide swift relief with the fewest side effects. While he waited for Rafaela to return with the medication, he flipped up his cell phone and arranged to have Sabrina's rental car delivered to his villa.

"We will leave the keys here at the clinic. Ah, here are your pills. They are very strong," he warned.

After she downed the correct dosage, Marco helped her into the wheelchair again. They made a stop at the woman's washroom, where Sabrina hopped in with Rafaela's assistance and out again a few moments later.

When he wheeled her out of the clinic and scooped her into his arms for the transfer to the Ferrari, he could tell she was already starting to feel the effects of the fast-acting medication. Her body was pliant in his arms, her breasts soft against his ribs. While he held her, she turned her face up to his.

"Thanks for taping me up, Doc. Duke. Marco."

Her smile was wide and natural. Nothing like Gianetta's teasing pout. He hadn't noticed the dimples before, perhaps because Sabrina Russo hadn't relaxed and smiled at him until this point. And her eyes were a warmer, richer brown than he'd first thought.

Holding her this close, her mouth just a whisper from his, Marco noted other differences, as well. Her breasts were fuller, her hips rounder and she had the long, sleek legs of a thoroughbred. She was much a woman, this American. Very much a woman.

Marco was more prepared this time when his groin went tight. Nevertheless, the punch hit hard and forced a reminder that this woman was his patient and would be a guest in his home. Willing his rebellious body to behave, he lowered her into the passenger seat and reached across her for the shoulder harness.

He smells like antiseptic soap, Sabrina thought, feeling more than a little woozy. Soap and suede and some subtle, tangy aftershave she'd only now noticed. She'd been too shaken—or too pissed—to sniff his neck before.

"How far is it to your villa?" she asked when he'd backed the convertible out of the clinic's courtyard.

"Not far. About five kilometers."

"Oh, boy! On these roads, that means we'll get there when? Midnight?"

"I promise, you'll arrive in plenty of time for a nap before dinner."

"I may zonk out before then," she warned as her head lolled against the seat back.

"I hope so." One corner of his mouth tipped up. "That will save much wear and tear on the floorboards!"

Despite the lethargy creeping through her, Sabrina registered the impact of that crooked grin. Holy crap! The man should come with a warning label. When he dropped his brusque me Doctor/you Jane attitude and let himself be human, His Excellency was downright dangerous.

"I'll try to restrain myself," she replied.

And not just her thumping foot, she admonished herself sternly. She couldn't let herself be distracted by sexy Italians right now. Caroline was depending on her for input into the megaproposal they had to submit by the end of next week. Sprain or nor sprain, crutches or no crutches, Sabrina intended to provide the required info.

For now, though, she'd just rest her head against the back of the seat and let the cool December air play with her hair. The loose tendrils fluttered around her face as the Ferrari maneuvered through the narrow streets of Positano.

The village was practically vertical. Pastel-painted shops and homes stair-stepped down the mountainside seemingly right on top of each other. At the bottom of the incline, dominating the piazza, was the cathedral. Beyond the church was the pebbly shore lined with colorful fishing boats.

As Sabrina had noted on the way into town, many of the small hotels and restaurants were shuttered. Umbrellas were folded and chairs neatly stacked on the terraces of open-air restaurants. Yet a few hardy tourists huffed up the steep, cobbled street, guidebooks in hand.

A momentary worry threaded through her as she wondered how the heck she'd handle streets like this on crutches, but she pushed the thought aside with a drug-induced optimism. She'd manage. Somehow.

When they left the town, the road once again became a narrow slice of pavement cut out of sheer rock. Rather than look down, Sabrina slumped in her seat and closed her eyes.

The next thing she heard was Marco's deep voice murmuring in her ear. "We're here. Don't stir. I'll carry you to your room."

She felt his arm slide under her knees. His other went around her waist. As if it was the most natural thing in the world, she wrapped an arm around his neck.

He lifted her easily. She could get used to this mode of transportation, she thought as she snuggled against his chest and buried her nose in the warm skin of his jaw.

"You need a shave," she complained sleepily.

"So I do. My apologies, Signorina. I'm on vacation, you see, and had not thought I would get this close to such a beautiful woman."

She nuzzled closer. "'S okay. You look good with bristles. You look good, period."

"Grazie."

She formed a hazy impression of a vine-covered arch, whitewashed walls, the sound of the sea slapping against rocks. Then a door opened and a gray-haired woman bustled out. Rafaela's mom, Sabrina thought as the woman greeted Marco in a torrent of Italian.

She heard him respond with her name, say something about ice. Mere moments later he lowered her onto sheets that smelled of sunshine and starch. His hands were gentle as he removed her one remaining boot. She was asleep almost before he propped a cushion under her injured ankle to elevate it.

Three

Food. She needed food.

The thought dragged Sabrina from a deep sleep. Or maybe it was the scents teasing her nostrils. Eyes closed, mind still only half engaged, she sniffed the air. The tantalizing aromas of garlic and onions sizzling in olive oil competed with something sweet and yeasty and fresh baked.

A loud rumble emanated from the vicinity of her stomach, reminding Sabrina she hadn't eaten since the roll and a cup of coffee she grabbed at the airport before claiming her rental car and driving south toward the Amalfi coast. She'd planned to stop at a restaurant along the way and lunch on the region's incredible seafood.

Instead, she remembered with a sudden jolt, she'd almost become food for the fishes!

The memory of how close she'd come to tumbling off a cliff and plunging into the sea brought her lids up. She blinked, confused for a moment by the unfamiliar surroundings, then the haze cleared.

She was in a bedroom. In Marco Calvetti's villa. Stretched out on a king-size bed. With her left leg stuck up at a thirty-degree angle and pillows propped under her knee and ankle. A cold compress was draped over the swollen joint.

She wiggled a bit to get comfortable and surveyed the room with more interest. It was a perfect blend of Mediterranean and modern, with Moorish arches and stucco walls painted a warm terra-cotta. An exquisitely carved antique chest stood against one wall. A flat-screen plasma TV hung on another.

But it was the view through the arches that held Sabrina spellbound. It gave onto a long, narrow terrace. Potted geraniums, hibiscus and trailing vines added splashes of color to an otherwise unbroken vista of sea and sky.

"Holy cow!"

Was that faint blur in the distance Capri? Sicily? Sabrina wasn't sure what part of the coast she was on or which direction the windows faced. She itched to get out onto the terrace for a better look and was gingerly lowering her foot when a soft knock sounded on the door behind her.

"Si," she called. *"Entri."*

"Good," Marco said when he opened the door. "You are awake."

"Barely."

She struggled to sit up as he came into the room. The first thing she noticed was that he was carrying a set of aluminum crutches. The second, that his sexy whiskers were gone.

Clean-shaven, his hair damp and slicked back, his broad shoulders molded by a cream-colored, V-neck sweater, he still looked good enough to eat.

Which reminded her…

"Please tell me that's Rafaela's mama's cooking I smell."

"It is indeed. I came to ask if you would like a tray here. Or are you feeling up to dinner on the main terrace? It is heated, so we'd be quite comfortable."

"You have another terrace with a view like this?"

"Several, actually. The villa is like the others along this stretch of coast. More vertical than horizontal, I'm afraid. But you don't need to worry about navigating stairs," he assured her. "I had an elevator installed when the place was built. The lift is very useful for Signora Bertaldi—Rafaela's mama. And for my own when she comes over from Naples for a visit."

"Then dinner on the terrace it is."

Now that she'd recovered from the shock of the accident and wooziness caused by the pills, Sabrina found herself intensely curious about the sexy doc.

"Does your mother visit often?" she asked as she pushed off the bed and onto her one good foot.

"Not often." He kept a firm grip on her arm while she experimented with the lightweight crutches. "Nor do I, for that matter. This is only my second time this year."

That surprised her. This bedroom didn't have an unused feel to it. The oversize marble tiles showed not a single dust bunny and light flooded through sparkling windowpanes. Rafaela's mama must have a squad of maids at her disposal to keep everything so fresh smelling and spotless.

"So where do you spend the rest of the year?"

"In Rome. That's where I have my practice."

Interesting. She knew now he had a mother in Naples and a practice in Rome. There were still some significant gaps in her database, however. Like whether there was a Mrs. Doc/Duke somewhere in the picture. Never shy, Sabrina figured there was only one way to find out.

"What about your wife? She must love coming down to this beautiful villa."

"My wife died three years ago."

"Oh, I'm sorry."

"So am I. Come, let's test your skill with these crutches."

His tone didn't invite further questions or expressions of sympathy. Sabrina swallowed her curiosity and clumped a few tentative steps.

"Be careful not to put too much pressure on your

armpits. You don't want to compress the nerves there. Use the foam handgrips to support yourself as much as possible."

He stayed close by her side her while she made a circuit of the spacious suite.

"Your rental car has been delivered," he said when he was satisfied she could maneuver. "Your cases are just outside, in the hall. Would you like me to bring them in so you can freshen up before we eat?"

"Yes, please."

She felt like she'd rolled in dirt, then gone to sleep in her clothes. Oh, wait! That's exactly what she had done.

"Can you manage alone, or shall I have Signora Bernaldi come help you?"

"I can manage."

"Very well."

He set her roller bag and briefcase on an upholstered bench at the foot of the bed and carried her smaller tote into the adjoining bathroom.

"There's a phone on the vanity and one by the toilet. Press one-six if you require assistance."

"One-six. Got it."

"I'll wait for you in the hall."

Sabrina fished in her suitcase for a black, ankle-length crinkle skirt and a velvet jacket trimmed with lace, then hobbled into the bath. The oval whirlpool tub drew a look of intense longing but she suspected she couldn't climb in without having to call for help climbing out.

Not that she'd mind getting naked with the doc. Especially now that she knew he was single.

Not single, she amended. *A widower.*

The thought of what he must have suffered sobered her.

She'd never lost a spouse, but had come close to losing her father when he was diagnosed with cancer several years ago. Foolishly, Sabrina had thought his illness might finally breach the walls between them. Instead it had left Dominic Russo more determined than ever to mold his only child into the woman he thought she should be.

She'd resisted his determined efforts for most of her life. With her mother watching helplessly from the sidelines, she and her father had engaged in a running battle of wills. Sabrina's warfare had taken the form of outrageous pranks and, later, wild parties.

His illness had sobered her, though. Shaken by his near brush with death, Sabrina had abandoned her own career as a top buyer for Saks Fifth Avenue and agreed to serve as the executive director of the Russo Foundation.

Big mistake. Huge. Her father couldn't give up an ounce of control. He'd questioned her decisions, countered her orders and generally made her life a living hell. She'd stuck it out, trying to make it work, until she finally admitted she could never fit the mold he'd designed for her.

Shaking her head at the memory of their titanic clashes, she thumped over to the vanity and sank down on a tufted stool. After stripping off her slacks and sweater, she went to work with a washcloth and lemon-scented soap before dragging a brush through her hair and reapplying her makeup.

The black crinkle skirt went over her head easily and dropped down to hide most of her bandaged ankle. The velvet jacket buttoned up the front, with a froth of ivory-colored lace swirling around the scooped neckline.

Feeling like a new woman, Sabrina dug in her suitcase for a pair of black, beaded ballet flats. She could only get one on, but its nonslip rubber sole provided an extra measure of security on the tiles as she crutched her way to the door.

Marco was waiting in the hall, as promised. Like the guest suite, the long, sunlit corridor sported graceful Moorish arches and a spectacular view of the sea. A magnificent Ming vase with a spray of fresh gladioli added to the fragrance of furniture polish and sunshine.

"The elevator's just here," he said, gesturing to a small alcove. "It will take us up to the dining room."

Up being the operative word, Sabrina saw when the door swished shut. The control panel indicated the villa was built on four levels. According to the neatly labeled buttons, the garage and main salon occupied the top floor. Below that were the library, the dining room and kitchen. Then came the bedroom level and, finally, the spa and stairs to what she presumed was a private beach.

"You weren't kidding about vertical," she commented as the elevator glided upward with silent efficiency.

"It is the price one pays for building where the mountains drop straight into the sea. Ah, here we are."

The elevator opened onto the library. It was a dream of a room, one Sabrina could happily have spent days or weeks in. Shelves filled with books and art objects lined three walls. The fourth wall was solid glass and gave onto another terrace with dizzying views of the ocean. Her crutches sank into a Turkish carpet at least an inch thick as she maneuvered around a leather sofa with a matching, man-size armchair and ottoman. What caught her attention, though, was the sleek laptop sitting atop a trestle table that looked like it might have once graced a medieval palace.

"Do you have wireless here?" she asked hopefully.

"I do."

"Mind if I use my laptop to log on?"

"Not at all. Here, I'll write the password for you."

He stopped at the table and jotted down a sequence of numbers and letters. Sabrina tucked the folded paper into the pocket of her jacket.

"Thanks. I think I mentioned I'm in Italy on business. I have several appointments I need to confirm. I also need to contact my partners. We're working a project with a very tight deadline."

"I understand. But first we eat, yes?"

"Yes!"

The mouthwatering scent of garlic and onions grew more pronounced as they entered the dining room. Like the library, this room, too, looked out on the sea. The table was a beautiful burnished oak and long enough to seat twelve comfortably. A smaller table had been set with china and crystal out on the terrace. It was tucked in a corner that protected it from the sea breezes and warmed by a tall, umbrella-like patio heater.

Lemon trees in ceramic pots provided splashes of color. Despite the lateness of the season, flowering bougainvillea climbed the walls. Enchanted, Sabrina passed the crutches to Marcos and eased into the chair he pulled out for her.

"I'll tell Signora Bertaldi we're ready," he said. "I would offer you an aperitif, but you should not combine alcohol with the drug I prescribed for you."

"No problem. The view alone is enough to get me high."

While Marco went inside, she breathed in a lungful of salty air and leaned forward to peer over the terrace wall.

Yikes! Good thing she wasn't acrophobic. She was sitting suspended in seemingly thin air, with only the wave-splashed rocks a hundred or so feet below.

Her host returned a few moments later with Rafaela's mama. "This is Signora Bertaldi. She runs this house—and me—with a most skilled hand."

The older woman blushed at the compliment. "His Excellency, he exaggerates."

Her eyes were dark and keen and set in a web of fine wrinkles. They stayed locked with disconcerting intensity on Sabrina's face.

"Please to excuse my English, Signorina Russo. It is not so good."

"It's better than my Italian. I met your daughter this afternoon, by the way. She says your *pesce spada* will make me weep with joy."

The strange intensity gave way to a wide smile. "Then it is good I cook the fish for you tonight, *si?*"

"Si."

"Please to sit, Excellency. I will bring the olives and antipasto."

Marco complied and stretched his long legs out. "So, Sabrina. Tell me more about this business that brings you to Italy."

She couldn't have scripted a more perfect finish to a day that had edged so close to disaster.

The sunset was glorious. The grilled swordfish was everything Rafaela had promised. The cappuccino came topped with sweet, creamy foam. The company…

Okay, she could admit it. She was seriously in lust with His Excellency, Don Marco Antonio d'Whatever. She'd always been a sucker for a man with smooth, polished manners and linebacker's shoulders. Not to mention tastes that ranged from opera to water polo to the succulent jerk-chicken skewers cooked up by New York City sidewalk vendors. And let's not forget eyes that crinkled at the corners when he smiled.

Still, she didn't deliberately plan her grimace as she got to her feet after their leisurely meal. Or her clumsy stumble when she tried to get the crutches under her. But she certainly didn't object when Marco muttered an oath and swept her into his arms.

"You're in pain, aren't you?"

"A little."

"I shouldn't have kept you up so long. You need to rest and elevate your ankle."

To hell with her ankle. A far more urgent need gripped Sabrina. With his mouth only inches from hers, she ached to brush her lips over his. She could almost taste their silky heat.

She didn't realize how transparent her thoughts were until they were in the elevator and he bent to press the button to take them to the lower level. When he straightened, he wore his doctor's face. Cool, assessing, concerned…until his gaze snagged hers.

Gesù!

Marco smothered the oath, but he couldn't hold back the hunger that punched through him, hot and swift and fierce. He wanted this woman. Wanted to taste her, touch her, hear her moan with pleasure as his mouth and hands roamed her lush, seductive curves.

The hours they'd spent together since their near calamitous meeting had erased his initial, absurd notion she might be Gianetta's twin. Or even, God help him, her ghost.

Sabrina Russo was nothing like his temperamental, tempestuous wife. Her laugh was spontaneous and natural, without a hint of frenzy lurking just under the surface. Her lively mind challenged his. And her mouth… Sweet Jesus, her mouth!

The elevator glided to a stop and the door slid open, but Marco made no move to exit. He knew he shouldn't yield to the urge to kiss this woman. She was his patient, a guest in his home. An American entrepreneur, impatient to be on her way and complete the tasks that had brought her to Italy. They were casual acquaintances at best. Strangers who would say goodbye in the morning.

The stern lecture proved completely ineffectual against the heat that raced through his veins. Only by an exercise of iron will could he hold off until he was sure she understood his intent. He saw it in the quick flare of her eyes. Heard it in the sudden rasp of her breath. With a low growl, Marco bent his head and took her mouth with his.

She tasted of dark coffee and sweet, rich cream. He angled his mouth, wanting more of her. Her arms locked around his neck. Her head tipped. She opened her lips, welcoming him, answering hunger with hunger.

He shifted her in his arms, his blood firing when her full breasts flattened against his chest. His body was so taut and straining with need he almost missed it when she gave a small jerk. He whipped up his head and caught her trying to cover a wince.

"Christ! I hurt you."

"No!" Her cheeks were flushed, her breathing ragged. "I banged my foot. The elevator…it's so small."

Shame and disgust hammered at him with vicious blows. Calling himself all kinds of a pig, Marco angled her injured foot away from the elevator wall.

"To kiss you like that was inexcusable of me," he ground out as he carried her into the corridor. His footsteps echoing on the tiles, he strode toward the guest suite. "I'm sorry, Sabrina."

The flush faded as her mouth tipped into a smile. "I'm not."

Still thoroughly disgusted with his lack of control, Marco shook his head. "I don't usually assault injured women."

"You don't, huh?" Amusement danced in her eyes. "How about those who aren't injured?"

"You tease, but that was no way for me—for anyone!—to treat a guest."

"Hey, you can't take all the credit, Doc. I was giving as good as I got back there in the elevator." She cocked a brow. "Or was I?"

He couldn't help but grin. "You were, Ms. Russo. You most definitely were."

That was still no excuse for his behavior. It took a fierce effort of will, but Marco managed to block the all-too-vivid feel of her mouth hot and eager under his and shouldered open the door to the guest suite. Signora Bertaldi had come down to straighten the room while he and Sabrina lingered over cappuccino. The bed was turned back, the sheets smoothed, the pillows plumped and ready.

Firmly suppressing the erotic and highly inappropriate thoughts that jumped into his head, Marco tugged down the top sheet and lowered his burden.

"We left the crutches upstairs. I'll ask Signora Bertaldi to bring them to you. She waited to help you prepare for bed before she left for the evening."

"Sure you don't want to tuck me in yourself?"

Laughter lurked behind her all-too-innocent expression. She was teasing him again. He knew it, but the knowledge didn't keep the gates from springing open and the mental images he'd just suppressed from pouring through. He could see her stretched out on those smooth sheets, one arm curled above her head, her lips parted in invitation…

Dammit!

"No," he admitted with brutal honesty. "I am not at all sure. But I'll send Rafaela's mama to you."

Marco was sweating when he left the guest suite. Shunning the elevator, he took the stairs to the upper floor. What the devil was wrong with him? Why did this woman stir such intense, erotic fantasies?

He hadn't remained completely celibate after his wife's death. He was a man. He had normal appetites, the usual physical needs. There were women in Rome, sophisticated women who played the game of flirtation and seduction with practiced charm. Yet none of them had roused him like this long-limbed American beauty.

Now he had to decide what the devil he would do about it.

Four

"Oh, yuck! Your ankle looks like an overcooked bratwurst."

Grinning at her friend's apt description, Sabrina swung the laptop propped on her stomach around. Its built-in camera made a dizzying sweep of the guest bedroom before her face was once again displayed on the screen alongside those of her two partners. How the heck had the world survived before videoconferencing?

"It is pretty gross," she agreed with a glance at her garish, yellow-and-purple lower limb. She'd unbandaged the ankle to let it breathe for a while. Before wrapping it up again and crawling under the covers for the night, she'd decided to try and contact her partners.

She'd caught Devon in Germany, where she was working frantically to set up the premerger meeting of executives from Logan Aerospace and Hauptmann Metal Works. Caroline, like Sabrina, was scouting sites for the job that had unexpectedly dropped into their laps last week.

"You need to stay off that ankle," Caro insisted, her heart-shaped face showing genuine concern. "Hole up at your hotel for the next few days and do not, I repeat, *DO NOT* even think about checking out those conference sites. I'll finish here and zip over to Italy. I can be there Thursday. Friday at the latest."

Devon countered with an alternate plan. "Don't cut your schedule short, Caro. I'll put things on hold here and fly down tomorrow. I can play nurse to 'Rina and scope out sites at the same time."

"Guys. Really. No need for either of you to charge to the rescue. I'll manage just fine."

"Sure you will," Devon scoffed. Her warm brown eyes held a combination of affection and concern. "I've been to the Amalfi coast. I know it's straight up and down. I also remember you mentioning that the hotel in Ravello had a lot of stairs and terraces."

"Actually, I'm not staying at the hotel. The doc who almost hit me offered to put me up at his villa tonight. He wants to check my ankle tomorrow to make sure I'm good to go before I take to the road again."

"That's the least the jerk can do," Dev huffed.

"Hey, did I mention that the jerk is a duke as well as a doc?"

Judging by their expressions, her partners weren't impressed.

"He's also seriously hot," Sabrina added nonchalantly.

The too-casual comment didn't fool either of her friends. They'd known her too long. They knew, as well, the good-time-girl reputation she'd worked so hard to maintain during her rebellious teen and college years.

Sabrina still enjoyed a good time. She wasn't particularly vain, but she recognized that her long legs and seductive curves attracted as many men as her family name and her father's wealth once had. As a consequence, she maintained a wide circle of male friends. Several had pushed to become more than friends. After so many years of resisting her father's attempts to dominate her, though, Sabrina was in no hurry to give up the freedom she'd struggled so hard to achieve.

That didn't mean she couldn't appreciate a real hottie when one almost ran her over. Especially one who could kiss like Marco Calvetti. She could still feel the delicious aftershocks of their session in the elevator.

"Uh-oh." Devon squinted into the camera at her end of the connection. "You've got that look on your face."

"What look?"

"The one that says your doc is fair game."

"Well, he is. His wife died a few years ago. I may be reading between the lines, but I think he's buried himself in his work since then. You wouldn't believe how gorgeous his villa is, yet this is only the second time this year he's driven down from Rome."

She chewed on her lower lip for a moment, mulling over her impressions of her host.

"He's really charming, guys, but also rather intense. It wouldn't hurt him to loosen up a little."

Devon and Caroline exchanged knowing, computer-generated glances.

"If anyone can loosen the man up," Dev drawled, "you can. Just remember you're now one of the walking wounded. Go easy on that ankle."

"And don't worry about scouting conference sites," Caro added. "Worst-case scenario, we can give Global Security fewer options."

"Absolutely not." Her professional pride stung; Sabrina was adamant. "This contract is too important. We're not scaling back our proposal. I'll be good to go tomorrow," she said firmly.

Which wouldn't give her time to loosen up the doc, she thought with real regret. Too bad. She could think of any number of inventive ways to follow up on that kiss.

Desire rippled through her as she said goodnight to her friends, shut down her laptop, and rewrapped her ankle. The damned thing still throbbed, but the ache was bearable so she decided against the pills sitting on the bedside table. Instead, she let the restless murmur of the sea surging against the rocks lull her to sleep.

She was up and dressed by eight the next morning. The faint scent of yeasty, fresh-baked rolls told her Signora Bertaldi was already at work in the kitchen.

Thankfully, Sabrina had stuffed a pair of merino wool palazzo pants in her suitcase at the last minute. The wide legs made getting them on over her still-swollen ankle a breeze. She teamed the oyster-colored slacks with a lightweight red sweater and a Versace scarf in a riot of colors. The rubber-soled beaded ballet slippers provided nonskid traction as she made her way along the tiled hall to the elevator.

She fully intended to hold the doc to his promise to check the sprain before she left. First, though, she intended to hold Signora Bertaldi to *her* promise of a goat cheese frittata for breakfast. If the frittata came anywhere close to the woman's grilled swordfish, heaven awaited on the floor above.

So did Marco, she discovered when she thumped into the library. He put aside the newspaper he'd been reading and sprang to his feet.

"You should have rung for help."

"I didn't need it," she replied when she recovered from the sight of the doc in well-washed jeans that hugged his muscular thighs and a silky black pullover that showed off some *very* impressive pecs.

Raising a crutch, she waved the tip in an airy circle. "I'm getting the hang of these things. What I *do* need, though, is coffee. Hot. Thick. Sweet."

"Of course." His assessing glance dropped to her foot. "But first, how is your ankle this morning?"

"Still fat and ugly, but it doesn't ache as much."

"Good. I'll look at it after we eat. Shall we have breakfast here in the library or on the terrace?"

"The terrace, please. I want to soak in every last ounce of your incredible view before I hit the road."

"I've been thinking about that." He matched his step to hers as they crossed through the dining room and went out on the spacious terrace. "I have a proposal for you to consider. Before I put it to you, let me fetch your coffee and tell Signora Bertaldi you are up and about."

Amused, Sabrina sank into the chair he held out for her and turned her face to the sun. She could get used to being waited on by a duke. Not that Marco fit her notions of royalty as shaped by her previous contacts.

She'd dated the playboy son of a Saudi sheik once. Just once. It was an eye-opening and not particularly pleasant experience. She'd also attended a couple of parties in London where Prince Harry popped in. He was great fun but way too young for her. Marco, on the other hand, was just the right age, height, size and shape.

Regret flickered through her. Too bad she was working against such a tight deadline. She wouldn't have minded a few more days with the sexy doc.

Maybe she could extend her stay in Italy after she finished checking out conference sites. Or arrange a return visit once they had the Global Security contract firmed up.

She was considering the possibilities when Marco returned with two cups of espresso topped with frothy cream. As he passed her one of the cups, he sprang the proposal he'd mentioned earlier.

"I think you should stay here for the rest of your time on the Amalfi coast. Use this villa as a home base and make day trips to the locations you want to check out."

The suggestion dovetailed so closely with Sabrina's thoughts she almost choked on her first sip of the thick, sweetened coffee. Her startled glance met Marco's calm gaze. If there was more than mere courtesy behind the invitation, he hid it well.

Her first instinct was to jump on the offer. Excitement pulsed through her at the thought of another session or two of close body contact with this intriguing man. Unfortunately, the road map she hastily conjured up in her mind quashed that quiver of excitement. The distances involved weren't all that great but she'd have to navigate them on tortuous roads, then gimp around on crutches.

"Thanks for the offer," she said with genuine regret. "It's very tempting, but I don't think I'm up to driving out and back each day on these roads."

"You don't need to drive them. I'll be your chauffeur."

"You?"

"*Si.*" A smile crept into his dark eyes. "Or don't you trust my driving? I would remind you that your foot did not thump the floorboards once during the drive from the clinic to the villa. Then again, you were out cold for most of that trip."

"You must have better things to do than transport me up and down the coast."

"Actually, I don't. I'm on vacation until January fifth. My surgical team has threatened to resign en masse if I return before that date. I have nothing on my schedule until then except a mandatory appearance at the ball my mother gives each year to celebrate La Fiesta di San Silvestro."

"That's on New Year's Eve, isn't it?"

"It is. So I'm at loose ends, you see. You would save me from utter boredom."

She didn't believe that for a minute. Someone with Marco's varied interests could easily fill up every minute of his vacation. His library alone could surely keep him occupied for weeks.

Sabrina hesitated, torn between the urge to spend more time with this man and the uncertainty of where it might lead. She didn't have time for personal entanglements right now. Caro and Dev were depending on her to provide the necessary input for the new contract proposal.

Which would be a lot easier to accomplish with someone who knew the area at the wheel, her traitorous mind pointed out.

That was a rationalization. She knew it. But what the heck. If the man wanted to spend his precious vacation time helping her nail down prospective conference sites, who was she to argue?

"If you're sure you have nothing more pressing to do," she said slowly, giving him a last out.

"I'm sure. And if you remain over until New Year's Eve," he added, "you must accompany me to the ball. It's really rather spectacular."

Okay, now she was hooked. What woman in her right mind would pass up the chance to attend a fancy-dress ball with someone like Marco Calvetti? The thought flashed into her mind that it was strange he didn't already have a date. The man was rich, cultured and a widower. But why look a gift hunk in the mouth?

"I'd planned to wrap up my business and fly home on the thirtieth," she told Marco. "I'll have to check on whether I can change my tickets. And get in some serious shopping. And…"

Signora Bertaldi's arrival with a loaded tray interrupted Sabrina's hasty revisions to her schedule. Tantalized by the mingled scents of broiled tomatoes, basil and melted goat cheese, she returned the older woman's greeting.

"Signorina Russo will be staying with us for a while longer," Marco informed her, speaking in English for the benefit of his guest. "You have additional help coming in from the village this morning, *si?*"

"Si, Excellenza." Signora Bertaldi placed the tray on the table. "The two who always assist me when you are in residence."

"Bring in more if you need them."

"I will," she promised as she positioned a heaping platter before Sabrina.

Marco himself poured fresh-squeezed orange juice from a carafe on the tray. The offerings also included a basket of fresh-baked rolls, a ramekin of creamy butter and an assortment of jams. Wishing them *buon appetito,* Signora Bertaldi left them to the dazzling sunshine and the sumptuous breakfast.

After breakfast Marco examined Sabrina's ankle. He had her sink into the soft leather of the sofa in the library and carefully unwrapped the Ace bandage. The swelling had gone down considerably but the skin was mottled with ugly purple-yellow bruises.

He rotated her foot gently, frowning when she fought to hide a grimace. "You really should stay off this today. It requires more ice and elevation."

"No can do. I need to get to work. How about I stretch out on the backseat of your Ferrari with an ice pack draped over my ankle?"

The prospect of driving around the Amalfi coast with a bandaged foot sticking out the rear window of his lean, mean machine didn't seem to particularly faze him, but he came up with an alternate suggestion.

"I have a better idea. My mother keeps a small fleet of vehicles at her home in Naples. I'll call and ask to borrow a sedan. It will give you more room and comfort."

"You're brave enough to tackle these hairpin turns in a big, honkin' sedan?"

"I've done it many times, I assure you."

"It will take you forever to get to Naples and back," Sabrina protested, remembering her own meandering journey after she left the interstate just south of the city.

"I'll have the car delivered. It will take an hour, two at most. During that time you will rest here on the sofa, with your foot up."

The command sounded so much like the ones her father used to issue that Sabrina bristled instinctively. Common sense kicked in a second or two later.

"Deal."

He rewrapped her ankle and helped her stretch out on the soft leather. Propping a pillow under her foot, he straightened and gestured toward the speakers attached to a high-tech iPod dock.

"Would you like to listen to some music while I fetch ice and make my calls?"

"What have you got on there?"

"Everything from Andrew Lloyd Weber to Zucchero."

Sabrina opted for show tunes over Italian pop rock. While Sarah Brightman and Steve Barton blended their voices in the haunting love duet from

The Phantom, she let her gaze roam the library. Until now she'd caught only brief glimpses of the room as she and Marco passed through it.

She took her time now, seeking clues to the personality of the man who fascinated her more by the moment. She couldn't make out the titles of the books in the shelves lining three walls and itched for a closer look. She settled for studying the treasures interspersed among the volumes.

That bust of a Roman matron looked as though it might have been carved while Pompeii was still a thriving metropolis. And that small oil painting on an ornate stand was either a Caravaggio or a damned good copy. A caduceus carved from translucent alabaster occupied place of honor amid a collection of objects that looked more like medieval torture implements than medical instruments. On the shelf next to the caduceus was a chess set with tall, elaborately decorated pieces in ivory and red.

Not until her gaze had made a complete circuit of the library did something begin to nag her. She couldn't put a finger on it right away. Frowning, Sabrina made another sweep of the bookcases before glancing at the long table that served as Marco's desk.

A maroon leather paper tray and blotter sat squarely in the center of the slab of polished oak. A gold Mont Blanc pen jutted from its holder beside the blotter. Next to it was his sleek laptop and a cordless phone propped up in its charger.

What was missing, Sabrina realized after another puzzled moment, were photographs. Most desks contained at least one, framed and positioned for optimal viewing. Usually of the owner's spouse or family.

Intensely curious now, she glanced around again. Nope. No snapshots. No formal portraits. Not even one of those cartoonlike caricatures sketched by the street artists who plied every piazza in Rome.

Apparently Marco didn't choose to surround himself with visible reminders of the wife he'd lost three years ago. Was her death still so painful?

Although intensely curious, Sabrina wouldn't poke her nose into his past. God knew enough people had poked into hers over the years.

Maybe he'd open up a little when they knew each other better. The prospect of spending the next few days getting to know the handsome doc had Sabrina humming along with Sarah Brightman.

Five

"You invited one of your patients to recuperate in your villa? An American?"

Marco smiled at the sniff that came through the phone. A Neapolitan born and bred, his mother had a native's disdain of foreigners. That included Sicilians, Sardinians and Corsicans as well as everyone west of the Apennines and north of the Abruzzi.

"Who is this woman?"

"Her name is Sabrina Russo. She's in Italy on business. Since I was partially responsible for her injury, I felt I should offer the hospitality of my home."

That touched on another sore spot. His mother understood why Marco preferred to stay at his own villa during his infrequent trips down from Rome instead of the palazzo in Naples his family had called home for generations. He still had apartments there, an entire floor. He and Gianetta had occupied the apartment most of their marriage, until Marco had accepted his current position as chief of neurosurgery at Rome's prestigious *Bambino Gesù* Children's Hospital.

Palazzo d'Calvetti was still his home, but these days he preferred the simple solitude of this villa he'd had constructed after Gianetta's death. His mother understood, but she didn't like it.

Marco dined with her regularly, which mollified her somewhat. And dutiful son that he was, he made the requisite appearances at her numerous charity and social events, including the big New Year's Eve gala. That reminded him…

"If Ms. Russo is still in Italy on the Feast of St. Silvestro, I'd like to bring her to your ball."

The request produced a startled silence. Marco understood his mother's surprise. He hadn't escorted any woman to the ball since Gianetta. With good reason.

The media had gone into a feeding frenzy after Gianetta's death. Even now the paparazzi hounded him mercilessly, and one disgusting rag insisted on trumpeting him as Italy's most eligible bachelor. He preferred to keep his private life private and was careful to avoid the appearance of anything more than casual friendship with the women he dated. Until now, that had meant *not* escorting any of them to the ball so steeped in his family's history and tradition.

Marco could rationalize the break with his long-standing policy without much difficulty. Sabrina would be in Italy for a short time. Her life and her business interests were on the other side of the Atlantic. At best, the attraction sizzling between them could spark only a brief affair.

But spark it would.

He'd already decided that.

He'd gone to bed last night hungry for this long-limbed American with the sun-kissed blonde hair and laughing eyes. The hunger hadn't abated after a restless night's sleep. Just the sight of her limping into the library this morning had given him an unexpected jolt.

She wanted him, as well. He'd seen it in her flushed cheeks and heard it in the flutter of her breath after their kiss in the elevator last night.

The memory of that urgent fumbling made him shake his head. He would handle her with more finesse next time, with more care for her injured ankle. He was plotting his moves when his mother recovered from her surprise.

"Yes, of course you may bring her. I'll have my secretary add her to the guest list. What is her name again?"

"Russo. Sabrina Russo."

"Russo." His mother sniffed again. "Her ancestors must have come from northern Italy. In the south, she would be Rossi."

"I don't know where her ancestors came from."

In fact, Marco realized, he knew very little about her other than she was in business with her two friends and in Italy to scout locations for a conference.

"Bring her to dinner," the duchess ordered. "Tomorrow. I want to meet her."

He returned a noncommittal reply. "I'll see if she's available and get back to you. *Ciao,* Mama."

"Tomorrow," his loving mama repeated sternly before hanging up.

He had to smile at the autocratic command. Maria di Chivari had married into her title more than forty years ago. Since then it had become as much a part of her nature as her generous heart and fierce loyalty to those she loved.

He reentered the library some moments later with a cold compress. Sabrina was lying on the sofa as ordered, her foot elevated, humming off-key to the mournful solo coming from the iPod. Mr. Mistoffelees, Marco identified absently, from the hit show *Cats.*

"The car is on the way," he said as he draped the compress over her ankle, "but I'm afraid I may have opened a Pandora's box. My mother wants to me to bring you to dinner tomorrow night."

"Is that bad?"

He answered with a rueful smile. "Only if you object to someone probing for every detail of your life, past and present. She has an insatiable curiosity about people."

"People in general? Or the women you invite to stay at your villa?"

Marco hesitated a few seconds before replying. "Other than a professional colleague or two, you're the first woman I've invited to stay."

He could see that surprised her. Shrugging, he offered an explanation.

"This place is my escape. My refuge. I had it constructed after my wife died. Unfortunately, I don't get down here often, and then only for short stays."

Her expression altered, and Marco kicked himself for mentioning Gianetta.

His guest didn't use the reference as a springboard to probe, but the question was there, in her eyes. He could hardly refuse to answer it, given the heat that had flared between him and this woman last night. He moved a little away from the sofa and shoved his hands in the pockets of his jeans.

"Before we moved to Rome, Gianetta and I lived in Naples. We kept a boat at the marina there. A twenty-four-foot sloop. She took it out one afternoon and a storm blew up."

His gaze went to the library's tall windows. The bright sky and sparkling sunshine outside seemed to mock his dark memories.

"Searchers found pieces of the wreckage, but her body was never recovered."

"Oh, no!"

The soft exclamation eased some of tension holding Marco in its iron grip. He'd heard so many platitudes, so many heartfelt expressions of sympathy, that they'd lost their meaning. Sabrina's soft cry was all the more genuine for being so restrained.

Inexplicably, he felt himself responding to it. With the haunting strains of Mr. Mistoffelees's lament in the background, he forced the memories.

"Gianetta loved to sail. Her family had made their living from the sea for generations. I used to joke she had more salt than water in her blood. She was—she was almost insatiable in her need to feel the wind on her face and hear the sails snap above her."

She had craved other thrills, as well. Downhill skiing on some of the Alps's most treacherous slopes. Fast cars. The drugs she'd flatly denied taking even after Marco discovered her stash.

At his insistence she'd gone through rehab. Twice. She swore she was clean, swore she'd kicked her habit. Yet he knew in his heart she'd driven down from Rome that last, fatal weekend to escape his vigilance. To escape him.

"I had a difficult surgery scheduled that week. A two-year-old child with a brain tumor several other neurosurgeons had deemed inoperable."

He'd been exhausted after the long surgery, mentally and physically, and wanted only to fall into bed. Gianetta flatly refused to cancel her planned trip to the coast. She'd been cooped up in the city too long. She needed the wind, the sea, the salt spray.

"I stayed in Rome until the boy was out of danger and in recovery, then drove down to join my wife for the weekend."

To this day Marco blamed himself for what followed. If he'd postponed the surgery… If he'd paid as much attention to his wife as he had his patients…

"I could see the storm clouds piling up when I hit the coast. I called Gianetta on my cell phone and begged her not to take the boat out."

Begged, cajoled, ordered, pleaded…and sweated blood when he arrived to find she'd disregarded his pleas and launched the sloop.

"As soon as I reached the marina, I contacted her by radio. By then she was battling twenty-four-foot swells and the boat was taking on water."

He could still hear her shrill panic, still remember the utter desperation and helplessness that had ripped through him. He could save the life of a two-year-old, but he couldn't save his wife.

"The last time I heard her voice was when she sent out an urgent S.O.S. The radio went dead in midbroadcast."

"How sad," Sabrina whispered. "You never got to say goodbye."

He flashed her a quick look, startled by her insight. For all their ups and downs, all the arguments and hot, angry exchanges, he'd never stopped loving his passionate, temperamental Gianetta. He'd sell his soul to be able to tell her so.

"You remind me of her," he said after a long moment. "You have the same color hair, the same eyes. Yesterday morning, on the road… For a second or two I thought perhaps I was seeing a ghost."

"So that's why you almost ran me over!"

Sabrina struggled upright on the sofa. She wasn't sure she liked being mistaken for a poltergeist, even briefly. And now that she thought about it, she realized Marco wasn't the only one who'd made that mistake.

"Now I know why Rafaela gaped at me at the clinic. Why her mama stared at me when I first arrived. Do I look that much like your Gianetta?"

His gaze roamed her face. "The resemblance is startling at first glance, but I assure you it's merely superficial. As I've discovered in the course of our brief acquaintance, Ms. Russo, you are very much your own woman."

"You got that right."

His slow smile banished the ghosts. "And very, very desirable."

Well! That was better. Mollified, Sabrina sank back against the cushions. She would have liked to draw Marco out a little more about his wife but she sensed his need for a shift in both subject and mood.

A quick glance at her watch indicated they still had some time to kill before the car arrived. She *should* get on her laptop. She needed to reconfirm her appointments for the next few days and update Devon and Caroline on the latest developments in her changing-by-the-minute schedule.

With Marco standing so close, though, Sabrina couldn't force her mind into work mode. Instead she nodded to the small, square table in the corner.

"I see you have a chessboard set up. We still have some time before the car arrives. Do you want to take me on?"

"You play?"

"Occasionally. When I do," she warned, "I usually draw blood."

"Ha!" He crossed to the table, lifting it with ease, and moved it into position beside the sofa. "We shall see."

Seen up close, the pieces drew a gasp of delight from Sabrina. They were medieval warriors from the time of the Crusades, with armor and weaponry depicted in exquisite detail. The Christian bishops carried the shields of fierce Knights Templar. The Muslim king was mounted on an Arabian steed. Even the queens wore armored breastplates below their circlets and veils.

"White or red?" Marco asked.

She chose white and saw that that the box containing the pieces also included a timer.

"The game will go faster if we play speed chess. How about two minutes max per move?"

When Marco nodded, she hit the timer to start the clock and moved a pawn in the slightly unconventional Bird's Opening, named for the nineteenth-century English master, Henry Bird.

Marco glanced up, his eyes narrowed, and countered with From's Gambit. Four moves later, Sabrina put him in check and had to bite her lip to keep from laughing at his stunned expression.

"You weren't joking about drawing blood. Who taught you to play like this?"

"My father. Chess is about the only thing we share a common interest in."

He lifted his gaze from the board. Sabrina deflected the curiosity she saw in his eyes by tapping the button on the timer.

"The clock's ticking. Your move, fella."

Frowning, he moved his rook to protect his king. She smothered a grin and countered with her knight.

"Checkmate."

Marco's brows snapped together. He scowled at the board, searching for another move, but she had him boxed in.

"I demand a rematch."

Sabrina took him three games to two and was about to put him in check again when the notes of a door chime cascaded through the intercom.

"That must be my mother's chauffeur. We'll finish this game when we return."

"Some folks are just gluttons for punishment."

While he went to trade car keys with the driver, Sabrina descended to the guest suite to slip on her jacket and grab her briefcase. The briefcase thumped awkwardly against her crutch as she hit the elevator again.

Marco was waiting when she emerged on the top floor. He'd pulled on his buttery suede bomber jacket and hooked a pair of mirrored aviator sunglasses in the neck of his black sweater.

Oh, man! Oh, man, oh, man, oh, man!

Suddenly, avidly eager to complete her business and get back to the villa, Sabrina let him take the briefcase and went through the door he held open for her.

She stopped just over the threshold. Her eyes widened when she took in the gleaming Rolls parked under the portico. "This is your mother's sedan?"

"One of them," Marco answered calmly as he opened the passenger door of the chrome-plated behemoth. "She likes to travel in comfort."

Sabrina was no stranger to limos or Rolls Royces. Her father never drove anywhere when he could be driven. This baby, however, was a classic. With its massive grill, elongated body and top folded down into an oversize trunk, it had been crafted before the automobile industry cared about such minutia as weight and fuel efficiency.

The prospect of taking the narrow, hairpin turns in this monster made Sabrina gulp. Resolutely, she quashed her nervousness and handed Marco the crutches.

"Do you have enough room?" he asked when she sank into cloud-soft leather.

"More than enough." She waved an imperious hand. "Drive on, McDuff."

Tourists of all nationalities had made the arduous ascent to the mountaintop town of Ravello for centuries. First by donkey cart, then by motorized vehicles, they climbed roads so steep and narrow that traffic had to back up in both directions to let a tour bus pass.

The views alone were worth the nerve-bending trip and the reason Ravello had drawn so many artists over the years. Their ranks had included D. H. Lawrence, who wrote *Lady Chatterley's Lover* while ensconced in a villa overlooking the sea, and composer Richard Wagner. Wagner's works had become the centerpiece of the town's annual music festival. The festival now drew thousands, according to the research Sabrina had done on the site.

Throughout the climb she caught awe-inspiring glimpses of sky and sea and rugged, rocky coast. The higher they went, the more stunning the vistas. Finally, Marco nosed the Rolls around the last steep curve and she caught her first view of the town itself. The twin towers of its cathedral dominated the jumble of whitewashed buildings perched high atop the cliff. Red-tile roofs and a profusion of flowering vines and trees added bright spots of color.

A sign indicated the town was closed to all vehicles except those belonging to residents and hotel guests. Another sign directed visitors to a parking lot at the base of the town walls. Marco bypassed the visitor lot and made for the main square. The Rolls bumped across the cobbled plaza crowded with tiny cafés, gelato stands and shops displaying beautifully crafted pottery.

The hotel Sabrina wanted to visit sat smack in the historic center of the town, almost in the shadow of the cathedral. When Marco pulled up at a facade adorned with weathered arches and belfry towers roofed in red tiles, a valet rushed forward to open Sabrina's door.

"Good morning. Are you checking in?"

"No, we're not staying," she replied in her shaky Italian. "I'm Sabrina Russo. I have an appointment with your hotel manager."

The well-trained valet switched to English as she swung out of the car. "Ah, yes. Mr. Donati, he says to expect you."

He supported her while she balanced on one foot, waiting for Marco to retrieve her briefcase and the crutches from the backseat.

"Do you wish a wheelchair, madam? I have one, just here."

"Thank you, but these are fine."

When she had the crutches under her arms, he tugged open the hotel's ornately carved door. "Please to go in and be comfortable. I'll call Mr. Donati to tell him you have arrived."

With Marco carrying her briefcase, Sabrina entered a lobby filled with light and terrazzo tiles and arches that opened on three sides to a courtyard with a magnificent view of the sea. In the center of the yard was a splashing fountain surrounded by lush greenery and tall palms nourished by the warm Mediterranean breezes.

They'd crossed only half of the lobby when a thin individual in a business suit and red-silk tie hurried out to greet her. He stopped short when he saw the man at Sabrina's side.

"Your Excellency! I didn't know… I wasn't aware…"

Flustered, he smoothed a hand down his tie and bowed at the waist.

"Please allow me to reintroduce myself. I am Roberto Donati, manager of this hotel. We met several years ago, when you and your most gracious mother opened Ravello's summer music festival."

"So we did. And this is Ms. Russo. She's come to survey your excellent establishment."

Donati took the hand Sabrina extended, obviously wondering how an American businesswoman had hooked up with the local gentry.

"Would you care for an espresso or cappuccino before we begin?"

"Perhaps later," she replied. "May I leave my coat and briefcase in your office while we tour the conference facilities?"

"But of course. Allow me to take them for you. And yours, Your Excellency."

Before handing over the briefcase, Sabrina extracted a pen and notepad. She skimmed her notes on Global Security's conference requirements and was ready when Donati returned with a folder.

"This contains our catering menus and the floor plans of our guest rooms and meeting facilities."

Marco took the folder. "You have your hands full, Sabrina. I'll carry this for you."

"Thanks."

With the men adjusting their pace to hers, she let Donati escort them across the open courtyard.

"Luckily, February is our off-season," the manager commented. "I indicated in my initial e-mail that we have fifty-three rooms available the week you specified. We've had several cancellations, so the number is now fifty-six. I have assurances from the hotel across the square that they can accommodate the remainder of your conference attendees."

"I'll want to see those rooms, too, before I leave."

"Of course. Once we finalize the meal plans, I'll provide a revised estimate incorporating those room rates."

"Hold on, I need to make a note of the numbers."

When she fumbled with the pen and pad, Marco stepped forward. "Let me do that for you."

She had to grin. "Doc, duke, chauffeur and secretary. You're a man of many talents."

His dark eyes smiled into hers. "Ah, but wait until I present my bill."

Damn! The man could melt her into a puddle of want without half trying.

Heat spreading through her veins, Sabrina handed him the pad and glanced up to catch the manager watching them. His goggle-eyed stare gave way to a combination of speculation and calculation.

Uh-oh! Maybe arriving at the hotel in a vintage Rolls with His Excellency in tow wasn't such a smart move. Good thing she had Donati's original estimate in writing. He'd better not try to pad the final figure. Sabrina would hold his feet to the fire.

She and Marco departed the hotel after lunch on a gorgeously landscaped terrace overlooking the sea. During the drive back down to the coast, she mulled over the revised estimate Donati had provided.

"How does it look?" Marco asked.

"The numbers seem high at first glance. I'll have to compare them to the final estimates from the other hotels."

"I'll call Donati and see if he can do better."

"No!"

Her sharp negative drew a surprised glance.

"Thanks," Sabrina said, tempering her tone, "but I prefer to handle these negotiations myself."

"My apologies. I merely wished to help."

She winced at the ice-coated reply. When he wanted to, the doc could wield one hell of a scalpel.

"Now it's my turn to apologize. It's just…"

She paused, chewing on her lower lip. The stubborn need to assert her independence had driven her for so long. She couldn't shake it, even now.

"My father doesn't believe I can make it on my own," she said finally. "I'm determined to prove him wrong."

"I see." Marco thought about that for a moment. "This is the father who taught you to play chess?"

"One and the same."

"He underestimates your killer instinct. I have your measure now, however. You won't win this evening as easily as you did this morning."

She couldn't resist the challenge. "Maybe we should up the stakes."

"Maybe we should. What do you suggest?"

Laughing, she waggled her brows. "Ever play strip chess?"

She was kidding. Mostly. And completely unprepared when Marco dug into his jacket pocket.

One handed, he flipped up his cell phone and punched a speed-dial button. His conversation was in Italian, but Sabrina caught enough to experience a sudden shortness of breath.

"The meeting took longer than anticipated," he informed his housekeeper. "There's no need for you to wait for our return."

He listened a moment and nodded.

"That will be fine. Thank you. I'll see you tomorrow. *Ciao*."

The phone went back into his jacket pocket. The slow, predatory smile he gave Sabrina told her the night ahead could prove extremely interesting!

Six

Marco lost one of his loafers in the first game. He forfeited its mate in the second.

"I've never seen such unorthodox moves," he protested. "You sacrificed a queen *and* a knight to gain a pawn."

"Thus opening the back door for my bishop. Stop whining and pay up."

He gave a huff of laughter and kicked off the loafer. As they reset the chess pieces for the next game, Sabrina calculated how many additional wins she'd have to score before she had him naked.

Socks, two.

Jeans, one pair.

One each belt, silky black pullover and, presumably, briefs.

Good thing they'd cut the two-minutes-per-move time limit down to one. Anticipation was putting her into a fast burn.

Anticipation, and the fact that they were alone in the villa. Stretched out on the plush Turkish rug in the library. With one of Vivaldi's violin concerti coming through the speakers and glasses of wine within easy reach. Since she hadn't had to resort to the painkillers after that first, powerful dose yesterday afternoon, she was enjoying the full-bodied red made from grapes grown in the Irpinia hills outside Naples.

They'd dispensed with the table and placed the chessboard on the carpet. Sabrina sat with her back against the sofa and her foot propped on a folded cushion. Marco sat cross-legged opposite her. He'd raked his fingers through his hair after one of her more outrageous moves. No longer neat and combed straight back, it showed more curl in the dark, disordered waves.

She itched to reach across the board and comb her hand through those waves. Or feather a finger along the dark sweep of his eyebrow. Or…

"Your move."

With a start, she saw he'd opened with queen's knight to a6. She advanced her king's pawn and the hunt was on.

* * *

She lost that game and paid with one of her beaded ballet slippers. They played to a draw on the next. Then Marco claimed her other shoe and she retaliated in the next game by crushing him with five moves.

"Ha! Take that!"

She expected him to peel off a sock or yield his belt. Instead, he dragged his black pullover over his head.

Sabrina's throat went bone dry. She'd snuggled against that broad chest each time Marco had carried her. Snuggling was good. She'd enjoyed snuggling. Seeing his upper half naked and in the flesh was better.

Her heart hammering, she let her gaze roam over the wide shoulders, the muscled pecs, the scattering of dark hair that swirled around his nipples and arrowed down toward his flat belly.

She didn't realize he'd deliberately sabotaged her concentration until she lost the next two games in a row. In the first, she forfeited her Versace scarf. She debated for several moments after the second.

What to surrender? Her slacks? Her red sweater? Or… Hmm. Her gaze dropped to the Ace bandage wrapped around her ankle.

"Don't even think it."

The amused warning brought her head up with a snap. Marco was watching her with the satisfied smile of a hunter who's cornered his prey. Her skin prickled everywhere his gaze touched.

"The bandage would be cheating."

"All's fair in love and strip chess, fella."

"In that case…"

With a quick sweep of his arm, he shoved the board out of the way. Sabrina started to protest the careless treatment of such beautiful pieces. The protest got stuck in her throat when Marco caught her elbow and slowly, inexorably, drew her down until she lay beside him on the silky carpet.

"Now, my beautiful Sabrina, I will claim my prize."

He slid a hand under the hem of her sweater. Her belly hollowed at the feel of his warm palm against her skin. Then his hand moved upward, tugging the sweater with it.

Cool air kissed her exposed flesh. So did Marco. She quivered as his mouth grazed her midriff, over the lace of her demibra, the mounds of her breasts. He tugged the sweater higher, and Sabrina raised her arms. The red knit came off, was flung aside. The hunger in his eyes stirred her to near fever pitch.

"I imagined you like this," he said, his voice rough. "Stretched out beneath me. Your arms above your head. Your mouth mine to take."

Suiting his actions to his words, he covered her mouth with his.

A flash fire ignited in Sabrina's blood. Her tongue met his. Her hands planed over his shoulders, his back, down the track of his spine. His skin felt smooth and hot over taut muscle and corded tendons.

They were both breathing fast when he fumbled for the front fastening on her bra. Sabrina retained just enough rational thought to gasp out a protest.

"You… You haven't won that yet."

"All's fair," he retorted with a wolfish grin.

The fastening gave and her bra went the way of her sweater. Marco's grin morphed into a look of such raw hunger that Sabrina's nipples tightened even before he bent to take one in his mouth. His teeth rasped the sensitive bud. His tongue soothed it. His teeth tormented her again.

Pleasure streaked from Sabrina's breast to her belly. Her back arched. She was hot and wet and ready long before he reached for the side zipper on her slacks.

He had her naked in less than a minute. When he rose to peel off his own clothing, her already erratic pulse went berserk. She almost licked her lips at the sight of his lean flanks and flat stomach. His sex, she saw with a jolt of fierce, primal elation, was hard and erect.

She reached for him, eager to wrap her hand around the steely shaft, but he turned away to drag the cushions off the sofa.

"We must take care, eh?" His accent thickening, he positioned her atop the cushions. "Your ankle…"

Sabrina was more concerned about other body parts at the moment. Like the aching tips of her breasts. And the spasms deep in her belly. And the wet heat between her thighs.

"Please tell me you have a condom somewhere close at hand," she begged.

The hunger in his dark eyes gave way to a flash of genuine amusement. "I'm Italian. What do you think?"

"I think," she panted, "we'd better stop talking and get the damned thing on."

He dragged his jeans over and extracted a packet from his wallet. *"Ecco."*

Sabrina snatched it out of his hands. "Let me."

He was all hard ridges and hot steel. So hard, she would have taken him in her mouth if she hadn't been desperate to take him into her body. So hot, she barely got the condom on before he jerked out of her hand and eased her back down onto the cushions.

Their first time was slow and careful.

Sabrina almost went mad at Marco's deliberate pace. In, out, in. Each insertion stretched her eager flesh. Every withdrawal left her panting for more.

She could feel her climax building. Feel the sensations spiraling outward from her core. Wanting to take him with her, she hooked her good leg around his thigh and clenched her vaginal muscles.

Every cord and tendon in his body went rigid. He gave a low grunt, but refused to thrust harder or faster. Instead, he wedged his hand between their straining bodies and pressed his thumb against her pulsing flesh.

Sabrina exploded in a flash of pleasure so intense the whole room seemed to rock. Marco whipped his hand away and surged into her. His body locked with hers, he rode her climax to his own.

Gradually, the room stopped spinning. Air rushed back into Sabrina's lungs. She looked up into the face a few inches from her own and gave a breathless laugh.

"Wow."

His mouth curved into a smug grin. "I think so, too."

They made love the second time in the shower.

Marco was afraid she might slip on the slick tiles and insisted on accompanying her into the spacious, walk-in enclosure.

He also insisted on soaping her down, front and back. She returned the favor. Mere moments later he had his shoulder blades planted against the tiles and Sabrina's thighs locked around his waist.

The third time came later, well past midnight.

Driven by a different kind of hunger, they invaded the kitchen. Sabrina was naked under the cashmere robe Marco had draped around her. He'd pulled on his jeans but hadn't bothered with a shirt or shoes.

She perched on a high swivel stool. Her elbows were propped on a counter made of tiles decorated with grape vines and baskets of lemons. Marco got out the seafood au gratin casserole Signora Bertaldi, bless her, had left in the fridge and slid it into the oven.

While they waited for the casserole to bubble, Sabrina munched on olives and tore pieces from a crusty loaf of bread to dip in oil and balsamic vinaigrette. Marco got out a corkscrew and another bottle of wine.

"Here."

She held up a fat black olive. Corkscrew and bottle in hand, he leaned forward, so she could pop it into his mouth. His strong white teeth just missed crunching down on her fingers.

"Mmm, good."

He set the bottle aside and dipped a crust of bread through the vinegar and oil mixture. Teasing, taunting, he drew the crust along her lower lip. Her eyes held his as she swiped her tongue over her lips and licked the drops of oil and sweet, tart vinegar.

His gaze locked on her mouth, Marco rounded the counter. Sabrina's borrowed robe gaped at her knees. He opened it further by the simple expedient of easing his hips between her thighs.

The next thing either of them knew, the oven was smoking and the seafood au gratin was bubbling over the sides of its dish in fat, sizzling splats.

Sabrina woke in Marco's arms the next morning. To her relief, she found the ache in her ankle had subsided to an occasional twinge and the swelling had almost completely disappeared. Gleefully, she abandoned the Ace bandage and traded the crutches for the cane Marco had delivered from the pharmacy in Positano.

While he showered, she slipped into a lacy camisole and a lightweight wool Emanuel Ungaro pantsuit, both in misty blue. Her ballet flats didn't do a whole lot for the outfit but she knew she wasn't ready for the three-inch heels on her only other pair of shoes.

They left shortly after breakfast for Sorrento and the first of the two facilities she intended to check out that day. The bustling harbor city had been a favored vacation spot since the days of Pompeii. Warm Mediterranean breezes made for streets lined with palm trees and a jumble of outdoor cafes. The balmy atmosphere provided an exotic backdrop for the colorful Christmas decorations still displayed in the streets and shop windows.

Sabrina craned her neck to take in the elegant nineteenth century facades of the hotels that had drawn so many visitors to this seaside resort. Only one had the available rooms and conference facilities to meet her client's needs.

The Excelsior Vittoria Grand Hotel sat high on the cliff once occupied by the Emperor Augustus's villa. With its fin de siècle buildings and magnificent views of Mount Vesuvius and the Bay of Naples, the hotel had played host to kings and queens as well as a long list of celebrities that included Enrico Caruso, Jack Lemmon, Marilyn Monroe and Sophia Loren.

Marco pulled up at its impressive portico and turned the car keys over to the parking valet. Sabrina had taken a lesson from the experience at Ravello. Concerned his presence might jack up the cost estimates, she asked him to enjoy a cup of cappuccino in the hotel's terrace café while she met with the assistant manager.

"Are you sure you don't wish me to help you take notes?" he asked, clearly amused by her stubborn determination to handle matters herself.

She countered with another question. "Have you attended any functions at the Excelsior?"

"Several," he admitted.

"Go." She waved a dismissive hand. "Relax. Have a cup of coffee."

"Very well. I'll wait for you on the terrace."

She met with the assistant manager in his office before taking a tour of the hotel's facilities. She had the quote he'd sent in response to her initial e-mail. After viewing the conference setup and finalizing meal selections, she bargained hard to get him to knock another ten percent off his bottom line.

Flushed with victory, she joined Marco on the sun-drenched terrace. He rose and slid his sunglasses down to the tip of his nose.

"I take it your negotiations went well."

"They did."

"Congratulations."

"Two sites down; two to go. At this rate, I'll have the information I need in plenty of time to prepare our final submission."

"I'm glad," he said, relieving her of her briefcase. "I was worried the accident may have impacted your ability to make your scheduled meetings."

"It would have," Sabrina admitted. "I couldn't have negotiated these roads or found my way around nearly as well without your help. Thank you."

"It's my pleasure."

His slow smile raised goose bumps up and down her spine.

"Very much my pleasure."

The day's second site survey required a trip by hydrofoil to the Isle of Capri. Like Sorrento, it had been a popular vacation destination since the time of the ancient Greeks. Its rocky cliffs rose from an azure bay, with resort hotels strung out along both sea level and the heights.

Sabrina had visited Capri's fabled Blue Grotto only once and would have loved to make a return trip. Unfortunately, they didn't have time to transfer to a small boat and ride the choppy waves into the cave. Her appointment with the manager of the hotel high on the cliffs overlooking the bay was set for two o'clock.

Marco accompanied her on the *funicolare* ride to the top of the cliffs. Good-naturedly he once again agreed to wait at a café in Piazza Umberto I. Sabrina wasn't as successful in her negotiations this time and almost wished she'd brought His Excellency along for additional firepower. Still, she left with a quote that was considerably under the one provided to her by the hotel in Ravello.

"Too bad," she commented to Marco on the hydrofoil back to Sorrento. "Ravello would have been my first choice. I liked the size of their break-out rooms and their audiovisual set up. Once I have the last estimate in hand, I might call Donati and see if he'll cut another five percent off his bottom line."

Stuffing her notes into her briefcase, she gave herself up to the vibrating hum of the boat's engine and the simple pleasure of Marco's arm draped over the back of her seat.

They'd left the Rolls parked at the ferry terminal. Marco held the passenger door for her and leaned down, his hand propped on the open door frame.

"How's your ankle holding up?"

"Good."

"Can you manage another stop?"

"Sure. Where?"

"My mother commanded me to bring you for dinner," he reminded her with a wry smile. "I can beg off if you wish."

"I'm fine. Really."

"Are you certain? I love my mother dearly, but she can be a bit overwhelming at times."

"Trust me. I learned at an early age to hold my own against overwhelming *and* overbearing."

He settled in the driver's seat and gave her a thoughtful glance as he buckled his seat belt. "You must tell me about this father of yours sometime."

"I will. Sometime."

But not with the sun sinking toward the sea and the early December dusk gathering on the hills. Right now Sabrina wanted to drink in the spectacular views of the Bay of Naples and enjoy the company of this intriguing, complex man.

"I'd rather you tell me about yours. I'd like to know a little about your background before I meet your mother."

"My father died when I was four. I barely remember him. I have a sister, AnnaMaria. She's an artist. She works mainly in bronzes and lives in Paris with her husband, also an artist. Perhaps you've heard of him? Etienne Girard?"

"I have! I attended an exhibit of his work a few years ago. His sculptures are, ah, very intense."

"Very," Marco agreed with a grin. "I'm still learning to interpret the message in rusted iron and neon."

"And your mother?"

"Ah, Mama." His smile turned affectionate and rueful at the same time. "She's Neapolitan born and bred. She has the blood of our history in her veins—Greek, Roman, Byzantine, Norman, Bourbon. Her father fought against the German military occupation during World War II and helped the city win its freedom in 1943. He was later elected to parliament, but was murdered by the Camorra because of his vigorous efforts to stamp out organized crime. They gunned him down on the front steps of his home."

His family had certainly suffered their share of tragedy. Like the Kennedys, Sabrina thought.

"After his death, my mother took up the fight herself. She, too, served in parliament until she married my father. Since then, she's used her title and her influence to help any number of causes."

"She sounds like a remarkable woman."

"She is."

Sabrina settled back in her seat, eager to meet the mother and learn more about the son who fascinated her more every hour she spent in his company.

Seven

As Marco explained during the short drive from the ferry dock, the original seat of the Dukes of San Giovanti was a hilltop fort north of Naples. The first duke received his title in 1523, along with his charter to guard the approaches to the rich trading port.

The present seat was a palazzo in the very heart of the city. To reach it, Marco negotiated the traffic-clogged harbor drive with a patience born of long familiarity. Sabrina didn't mind the slow crawl. It gave her plenty of opportunity to gawk at the massive fortress guarding the harbor. Begun by the Angevins in the eleventh century and added to by the Spanish in subsequent centuries, the castle served as royal residences for a long succession of kings.

She also got glimpses of the famous Quartieri Spagnoli—the Spanish Quarter, laid out by Spanish soldiers in the seventeenth century. The teeming, densely populated area was quintessential Napoli.

Tall, multistory stucco buildings crowded so close together that the balconies on one side of the street almost touched those on the opposite side, completely blocking out the sun. Washing flapped from the balconies like bright pennants. The colorful Christmas decorations strung across the narrow alleys added to the chaotic scene.

Sabrina spotted a crew taking down the Christmas decorations and replacing them with a banner announcing a massive fireworks display and rock concert to celebrate the coming Fiesta di San Silvestro.

"I bet the Spanish Quarter rocks on New Year's Eve."

Marco flicked a glance at the dark tunnel of streets. "You don't want to wander into the Quarter at night. Especially the night of San Silvestro. Some Neapolitans still practice the tradition of throwing broken furniture out the window to show they're ready for a fresh start."

"Out with the old, in with the new, huh?"

"Exactly." He maneuvered around a traffic circle and turned onto a wide boulevard. "We have another tradition you may want to consider, however. Wearing red underwear on New Year's Eve is supposed to bring good luck."

His smile was slow and wicked.

"I would enjoy seeing you in red underwear. I would enjoy even more getting you out of it."

"Then I'll have to hit the shops," Sabrina said, laughing. "Red panties and a dress for your mother's New Year's Ball. *If* I get everything done I need to and can change my airline reservations."

"We will get it done."

"We have New Year's traditions in the States, too," she commented as the boulevard sloped up toward the magnificent baroque cathedral dominating the city's skyline. "When you did your residency in New York, do you remember champagne toasts and black-eyed peas on New Year's Day?"

"I remember more the nonstop football games. Or what you American's call football."

"What about resolutions? Do you make 'em and break 'em like we do?"

"That's an all-American tradition." He threw her a quick look. "Have you made yours for the coming year?"

"Not yet. I'll have to think about it."

She didn't have to think long.

She'd intended to fly home late tomorrow evening. Even if she changed her ticket, she would gain only a few more days in Italy. Marco had to return to Rome by January fifth and she needed to be back in the States by then, working furiously with Caroline to put their final proposal together for the Global Security conference.

She wouldn't think about the ticking clock, Sabrina resolved. She'd enjoy the time she had left in Italy. She'd scout the last hotel, stuff herself on Signora Bertaldi's cooking, go to a ball and make love morning, noon and/or night to her handsome doc.

With that delicious resolution firmly in mind, she craned her neck for a better view of a fat, white moon rising above the cathedral's spires.

Sabrina fell instantly in love with the Palazzo d'Calvetti.

Three stories tall and at least eight bays wide, its facade featured different window frames and pediments on each level. She could see the Moorish influence in some, the Italian Renaissance in others. A crowning cornice topped by statues of various saints ran the length of the facade.

Marco parked under a central portico supported by marble columns and escorted Sabrina up the shallow front steps. They were met at the door by a butler who welcomed His Excellency home with genuine warmth.

"*Grazie,* Phillippo. This is Ms. Russo, my guest."

The butler blinked in surprise but recovered quickly. "*Buona sera,* madam."

Sabrina was starting to get used to these double takes and answered with a smile. "*Buona sera.*"

"Is my mother in the main salon?" Marco asked.

"She is, Your Excellency, but she wished me to

let her know the moment you arrived and she will come down."

While he pressed a buzzer on the intercom panel, Sabrina took in the magnificent barrel-vaulted main hall lavishly decorated with hand-painted Majolica tiles. A grand staircase bisected the hall in dead center and led in sweeping twin spirals to the upper floors.

She was still absorbing the rich architectural detail when a door slammed on the second floor. A moment later, a slim, silver-haired woman in tailored slacks and a mink-trimmed sweater hurried down the stairs.

"Marco!"

"Buona sera, Mama." Bending, he kissed her on both cheeks. *"Come sta?"*

"Bene. Multo bene."

The affection between the two was genuine and readily apparent, but when the duchess turned to his guest her warm smile vaporized.

"Madre del Dio!"

Sabrina suppressed a sigh. Marco had assured her the resemblance to his dead wife was merely superficial. She was beginning to wonder. He covered the awkward moment with an introduction.

"Sabrina, may I present my mother, Donna Maria di Chivari Calvetti. Mama, this is my guest, Sabrina Russo."

"Forgive me for staring," the duchess apologized in musically accented English. "It's just… You look much like…"

"Like Gianetta," her son finished calmly. "At first glance, I thought so, too. But you will find, as I have, it is only a trick of the eye."

An odd expression flickered across his mother's face. It came and went so quickly Sabrina couldn't interpret it. She had no difficulty interpreting the cool comment that followed, though.

"I will admit I was surprised when my son told me he had a guest staying at his villa." She raked a glance at said guest from her windblown hair to the tip of her cane. "I hope you're recovering from your unfortunate accident?"

The question was polite, but the slight if unmistakable emphasis on the last word almost made *Sabrina* do a double take.

Good grief! Did the woman think she'd tumbled down a cliff in a deliberate attempt to snare her rich, handsome son? Had that—or some similar ploy—been tried before? She'd have to ask Marco later.

"I'm recovering quite well, Your Excellency. Your son has taken excellent care of me."

She would have loved to add that his bedside manner was improving every day, too. Wisely, she refrained.

"Indeed."

With a regal nod, the duchess led the way past the marble staircase to the west wing of the palazzo.

"I wasn't sure you'd be able to mount the stairs so I've ordered an aperitif tray to be set up in the Green

Salon. It's on this floor and there's a water closet just there, across the hall, if you wish to use it."

"Thank you, I do."

"We'll wait for you in the salon," Marco said. "It's the third room on the left."

Sabrina didn't dawdle. Her lip gloss and hair restored to order, she left the powder room and counted the rooms as she passed them. The first looked like it might have been once been the palazzo's armory and now served as a museum for antique weapons displayed in locked cases. The second was an office of sorts, with glass-fronted cabinets containing tall, leather-bound volumes of documents. Sabrina's partner, Devon the history buff, would salivate at the sight of those musty volumes.

"…do you know about her?"

The duchess's sharp question came through the open door of the third room, as did Marco's reply.

"I know enough, Mama."

The exchange was in Italian but clear enough for Sabrina to follow easily. She took another step before she realized her soft-soled flats and the rubber tip of her cane masked her approach.

"You say she's in Italy on business?"

"She and her partners provide travel and support services for executives doing business in Europe. She's scouting conference sites."

Time to announce her presence, Sabrina thought. She lifted the cane, intending to thump it on the parquet floor. The duchess's next comment stopped her cold.

"If half the articles my secretary pulled off the Internet about this woman are true, she's scouting more than conference sites."

"What do you mean?"

"She's the daughter of Dominic Russo, the American telecommunications giant. He put her on the board of the foundation that oversees his charitable interests, but subsequently removed her. The rumor is he's disinherited her. Cut her off without a cent."

"Ah," Marco murmured. "So that's why she's so determined to make it on her own."

"Perhaps, perhaps not. Don't you think it's just a little too coincidental that she fell right at your feet?"

Sabrina had heard enough. Bringing the cane down with a loud thud, she entered the salon.

Marco stood behind a tray holding an array of bottles, a silver martini shaker in his hand. His mother was seated in a tall-backed armchair and had the grace to appear chagrined for a moment. But only for a moment. Her chin lifted as Sabrina gave her a breezy smile.

"Your information's accurate, Your Excellency, except for one point. My father didn't remove me from the board of the Russo Foundation. I quit. Are those martinis in that shaker, Marco?" she asked with cheerful insouciance. "If so, I'll take two olives in mine."

"Two olives it is," he confirmed with a gleam of approval in his dark eyes.

His mother was less admiring. "I'm sorry if I offended you, Ms. Russo," she said coolly. "I wish only to watch out for my son's welfare."

"I understand, Your Excellency. No offense taken."

"I'm perfectly capable of watching out for my own welfare," Marco drawled as he handed his mother a tall-stemmed martini glass. "But I thank you for your concern."

The duchess merely sniffed.

She unbent a little over dinner served in a glass-enclosed conservatory that looked out over the lights of the city.

"Have you visited this part of Italy before, Ms. Russo?"

"Only once, when I was a student at the University of Salzburg. One of my roommates was a history major. We drove down from Austria one weekend to explore the ruins at Pompeii and Herculaneum."

"So you've not spent time in Napoli."

"No, Your Excellency."

"You must call me Donna Maria."

Sabrina's lips twitched at the royal command. "Certainly. And please, call me Sabrina."

"We have a painting by Lorenzo de Caro in the gallery. It depicts the city as it was in the early eighteenth century. You must let me show it to you after dinner."

The rest of the meal passed with polite queries concerning Sabrina's year in Salzburg and her current business. Not until she and the duchess had made their way to the galley, leaving Marco to look over a document his mother wanted his opinion on, did she learn the ulterior motive behind the invitation to view de Caro's masterpiece.

The painting was small, only about twelve by eighteen inches, but so luminous that it instantly drew the eye. Lost in the exquisitely detailed scene of a tall-masted ship tied up at wharf beside the fortress, Sabrina almost missed Donna Maria's quiet question.

"How much has my son told you about his wife?"

"Only that she died in a tragic boating accident. If Marco wants me to know more," she added pointedly, "I'm sure he'll tell me."

The duchess hiked a brow. "You are a very direct young woman."

"I try to be, Donna Maria."

"Then I will tell you bluntly that I love my son very much and don't wish to see him hurt again."

"I don't plan to hurt him."

"Not intentionally, perhaps." Her forehead creasing, the duchess studied her guest's face. "But this resemblance to Gianetta..."

"It can't be that remarkable," Sabrina said with some exasperation.

"Come and judge for yourself."

Donna Maria led the way to the opposite wing

of the gallery. It was lined with portraits of men and women in every form of dress from the late Middle Ages onward. Cardinals. Princesses. Dukes and duchesses in coronets trimmed with fur and capped with royal red.

"These are my parents." She stopped in front of a portrait depicting a willowy blond and a stern-looking man in a uniform dripping with medals. "And here are my husband and I in our wedding finery."

The painter had captured the couple in the bloom of youth. There was no mistaking the love in the young Donna Maria's eyes or the pride in her husband's as he gazed down at her.

"How happy you both look."

"We were," the duchess said softly.

Her gaze lingered on the portrait for a long moment before moving to another. This one showed her seated on a garden bench with her two children standing beside her.

"This is Marco at the age of eight, and my daughter AnnaMaria at age six."

Sabrina could see the man Marco would become in the boy's erect posture and intelligent eyes.

"And this is Gianetta," the duchess said, her tone hardening. "Marco had this painted shortly after they were married."

Unlike the other portraits in the gallery, this one was an informal collage of sky and sea and sail. At its center was a windblown, laughing woman manning the helm of a sleek boat. The colors were vivid, the strokes bold slashes of sunlight on shadow.

Disconcerted, Sabrina leaned forward for a closer look. She might have been looking at a portrait of herself in her younger, wilder days. The hair, the eyes, the angle of the chin… No wonder everyone close to Marco gawked when they saw his houseguest!

"She was beautiful," the duchess said, making no effort to disguise her bitterness. "So beautiful and charming and unpredictable that everyone fell all over themselves to find excuses for her erratic behavior. Everyone except me. I could never… I *will* never forgive her for putting my son through such hell."

Whoa! That was a little more information than Sabrina had anticipated. Donna Maria didn't give her time to process it before zeroing in for a direct attack.

"Is the resemblance between you and Gianetta more than physical, Ms. Russo? Are those other stories my secretary pulled from the Internet true?"

Sabrina's eyes narrowed. "As I said earlier, you shouldn't believe everything posted on the Internet."

The duchess refused to be fobbed off. Like a lioness protecting her cub, she went straight for the jugular.

"Which story isn't true? The one that claims you seduced the son of a sheik? The one that says you like to party until dawn at nightclubs in New York and Buenos Aires and London?"

The gloves were off now, Sabrina thought grimly.

Like they'd been so many times with her father. Well, she was older and a whole lot wiser this time around. The body blows didn't hit as hard or hurt as badly as they did when her father threw them.

"Sorry, Your Excellency." Her shrug was deliberately careless. "I'm well past the age of having to defend my actions. To you or anyone else. Shall we join Marco for coffee?"

With Sabrina's ankle so improved, Marco returned his mother's Rolls and reclaimed his Ferrari. The powerful sports car ate up the miles between Naples and his seaside villa in less than an hour.

Sabrina was quiet for most of the trip, more shaken than she wanted to admit by the exchange with his mother. Her past had come back to haunt her with a vengeance. All those wild parties… All those torrid affairs… She couldn't deny them and was damned if she'd try.

She wondered whether the duchess had poured the juicy stories into her son's ears. Marco gave no sign of it when he accompanied her to the guest suite.

Or when he took her in his arms.

Or when his mouth came down on hers.

The heat was instant and so intense Sabrina knew she was in trouble. Her bones had never liquefied like this. Her blood had never bubbled and boiled. She wanted this man more with each breath she took but, somehow, found the strength to ease out of his embrace.

"Your mother showed me Gianetta's portrait. She looked so vibrant. So full of life."

"She was," he said simply. "I loved her with all the passion of my youth."

Sabrina hugged her waist. She'd tasted passion, too. Many times. But with the brutal clarity of hindsight, she saw that she'd never truly loved. Not the way Marco described.

She could love this man, though. She knew it, deep in her heart. She was already halfway there.

She was still dealing with that disconcerting realization when he unbelted the jacket of her pantsuit and undid the buttons, one by one.

"Ah, Sabrina."

He dipped his head and kissed her nose, her mouth, her chin, the swell of her breasts above the lacy chemise.

"You enchant me," he murmured in Italian, his voice low and rough. "You enthrall me. You make me feel alive again."

Eight

"He said that?"

Amusement rippled across Caroline's heart-shaped face, displayed next to Sabrina's on the laptop's screen.

"You enthrall him?"

"It didn't sound as corny in Italian."

Sabrina scooted up a little higher and balanced the computer on her bent knees. She'd decided to laze amid the rumpled sheets and duvet while Marco showered. After the night just past, she wasn't sure she'd have enough strength to roll out of bed and take her turn.

At least she'd managed to reach over the side of the mattress for his discarded shirt and pull it on before powering up the computer. She could smell the faint tang of his aftershave mingling with the scent of their lovemaking as she queried her partner.

"Are you sure you don't mind if I stay in Italy until January fourth, Caroline? That's the first day I can get out on a new ticket."

It was also the *last* day she could spend with Marco before he headed back to Rome. Sabrina shoved that nasty thought aside. They still had today and the Feast of San Silvestro tomorrow and New Year's Day and…

Caroline interrupted her mental count. "Of course I don't mind. I won't get home until late on the third myself. Zap me your estimates and I'll send you mine. We can do the comparative analysis by e-mail and work up the final proposal when we get home."

"Will do. I just have one more site to check out. Marco and I are going to hit it today. Then I have to do some serious shopping."

"For?"

"A ball gown."

"You're going to a ball?"

"Yep. We're going to celebrate the New Year in style."

"Answer me this, my friend. How will you dance on that ankle?"

Sabrina raised her leg and examined the joint in question.

"The swelling's gone. I can actually see the bones again. They're still covered in ugly green and purple, but what the heck. Here, have a look."

She swiveled the laptop around and aimed the built-in camera at her foot.

"The pain is gone, too," she said, wiggling her toes. "If I take it easy and use the cane today, I ought to be able to manage at least one waltz tomorrow night. Although…"

She repositioned the laptop and saw her own face screwed up in a grimace.

"I was pretty ambivalent about attending the big bash after meeting Her Excellency yesterday."

"What changed your mind?"

The grimace morphed into a catlike grin. "Marco. The man can be pretty convincing when he wants to."

Her partner smiled but still had doubts. "From what you told me about his mother, I have to say she sounds rather formidable."

"She is."

Caroline bit her lip. She and Devon knew all too well the scars Sabrina had acquired over the years in her fierce battles with her father.

"You've spent a good part of your life fighting to hold your own against a domineering parent. Are you sure you want to enter into battle with another?"

"I'm not engaging in a protracted battle. I'm just attending a party with my studly doc-slash-duke, after which we'll go our separate ways."

She shrugged aside the disconcerting twinge that caused and cocked her head.

"The shower just cut off in the bathroom. Gotta go, Caro. I need to confirm the ticket change, get dressed and hit the road. I'll e-mail a spreadsheet with the final cost estimates for the sites here in Italy as soon as I nail down the last one."

"Okay. I'll do the same for the sites in Spain."

"*Ciao* for now, girl."

She ended the videoconference and sent her fingers flying over the keyboard. She'd have to pay a hundred and eighty dollar differential in airfare plus another hundred in penalties for changing her ticket. Add in the cost of a gown and the necessary accessories, and this was turning out to be an expensive stopover.

Since these weren't business-related expenses, Sabrina intended to cover them from her personal account. Good thing she'd built up a healthy savings before walking away from the board of the Russo Foundation.

Marco emerged from the bathroom just as she clicked the confirm button to purchase the new ticket. "It's done. I've changed my… Yowza!"

She froze with her fingers still curved over the keyboard, speechless at the sight of six foot one of nearly naked male.

He had a towel draped around his hips. Above the fluffy cotton his chest hair gleamed dark and damp. Below, his muscular thighs narrowed down to strong calves and disgustingly healthy ankles. With his bronzed skin and short, curling hair, he could leave a string of broken hearts from Naples to Nashville to Nepal.

"You should give a girl some warning before you stroll into a room looking like that! I almost swallowed my tongue."

"Tongue swallowing could be symptomatic of a serious medical condition," he said solemnly. "You'd better let me have a look."

He had to drop the towel in order to make the necessary examination. For some reason, he also had to peel off Sabrina's borrowed shirt.

The laptop got shoved onto the bedside table. The duvet slithered over the side of the mattress. Marco curled his hands under her thighs and tugged her down until she was stretched out under him.

"Open your mouth and say ah."

"Now that," Sabrina gasped when they came up for air some time later, "was what I call a thorough examination. I might have to hire you as my personal physician."

Marco rolled onto his side and propped his head in his hand. Christ, she was beautiful. With her tangle of tawny hair and her long, supple body lying limp beside his, she made him feel smug and sated and hungry, all at the same time.

"It would be difficult for me to make house calls to the States. You'd have to stay here, in Italy."

He said it with a lazy smile but as soon as the words were out the idea took hold. Suddenly thoughtful, he let his gaze drop to her mouth, still swollen from his kisses, and brought it up to meet hers again.

"Why *not* stay longer, Sabrina?"

"I wish I could. Unfortunately, my partners and I have a company to run."

Marco curled a tendril of tawny gold around his finger and feathered the ends with his thumb. Just a few days ago he'd driven down from Rome with nothing more than a week of rest and relaxation in mind. Then this woman had dropped into his life. They'd spent less than a week together, but all he had to do was look at her to know he wanted more.

"Since your company provides support for executives doing business in Europe," he said slowly, "perhaps you should consider the cost effectiveness of establishing a forward operating location in, say, Rome."

Chuckling, she dropped a kiss on his chest. "That would certainly make house calls more convenient for my personal physician. Now I suggest we postpone any further doctor/patient consultation until later. We gotta get it in gear, fella."

Marco let the subject drop, but the idea of keeping Sabrina in Italy remained fixed in his mind during the drive to the last conference site on her list, a resort some forty kilometers south of Salerno.

The Villa d'Este sat all by itself on a rocky promontory jutting into the sea. It was a new condo/time share/vacation resort that had been constructed for guests who wanted to avoid the bustle of the more popular tourist locales. The facilities were top rate and the prices comparable to the other sites Sabrina had scouted, but she left ready to cross the place off her list.

"Too isolated and difficult to get to," she commented as the Ferrari slowed for a truck spewing a black cloud of diesel fumes. "Good thing I made a previsit. On paper, the resort looked perfect."

With a blind curve ahead, Marco couldn't pass. He dropped back, his nostrils flaring at the noxious fumes.

"So, which of the other three locales tops your list?"

She flipped through her notes. "I really liked the facilities and unique setting in Ravello, but that estimate came in considerably higher than either Sorrento or Capri. I e-mailed Signor Donati yesterday and asked him to take another look at his catering costs."

Marco didn't offer to weigh in with Donati. He'd made that mistake once, and felt the bite of Sabrina's prickly independence. Yet he knew one phone call from him could resolve the issue.

The knowledge bothered him. He wasn't used to sitting back while someone else took the lead. He headed a highly skilled surgical team with unquestioned authority. He made life and death decisions daily in the operating theater, and made them fast. In addition to chairing the neurosurgery department at his hospital, he sat on the board of directors for the International Pediatric Neurosurgical Association and the Gamma Radioknife Institute. He routinely loaned his name, his title and his reputation to any number of charitable enterprises. That combination carried as much weight here in southern Italy as it did in Rome.

At Sabrina's specific request, however, he'd stayed in the background while she met with the hotel personnel in Capri, Sorrento and at the Villa d'Este. He'd shrugged off her stubborn determination to handle matters herself at the time. Now it put a decided dent in his ego. She was foolish not to use his influence, he thought as the truck in front of them belched another wave of noxious fumes.

Muttering a curse, Marco pulled out to pass. A long line of oncoming cars forced him to cut back.

"At this rate, we'll eat his exhaust all the way back to Salerno."

The irritated comment drew a quick glance from the woman beside him. She stuffed her notes in her briefcase with a rueful smile.

"I told you before, but I'll tell you again. I really appreciate you playing chauffer for me this week."

Marco didn't want her appreciation. He wanted her. The more he thought about keeping her in Italy, the more determined he was to make it happen.

He needed to lay some groundwork first, and he couldn't do that with this damned truck spewing fumes in his face. He caught sight of a brown sign ahead denoting the turnoff for a place of historical interest.

"Have you been to the Temple of Poseidon at Paestum?" he asked as the sign flashed by.

"No."

"It's too close by for you to miss."

"Marco, we don't have a lot of time for sightseeing. It's almost three o'clock now and we're still several hours from home."

He slowed for the turn and cut the wheel. "This won't take long."

Sabrina stifled a dart of annoyance. After his good-natured chauffeuring, she could hardly insist they save Paestum for another day.

Still, she couldn't help thinking of all she needed to get done. At the top of the list was putting her notes in order and e-mailing Caroline the results of her site surveys. When she received the input from Caro's surveys, she'd have to get to work on a comparative analysis. And sometime before the ball tomorrow night she needed to squeeze in a few hours of shopping. The last thing she was interested in right now was a side trip to view some ruins.

Her minor annoyance evaporated at her first glimpse of the temples. The three massive Doric structures rose from a grassy plain dotted with the scattered remnants of the ancient city built by the Greeks around 600 B.C.

"The one in the center is as large as the Parthenon!" she gasped. "And so beautifully restored."

She got a better view of the main temple when they pulled into the visitor's parking lot. Awed, she let her gaze roam the starkly beautiful rows of columns topped by an elaborate frieze and a pitched roof. Marco hooked an arm over the steering wheel, content to sit for a few moments while she absorbed the incredible sight.

"The center temple was dedicated to Poseidon," he told her. "The god of the sea. He was known as Neptune to the Romans, who took the city from the Greeks and occupied it until well into the ninth century."

"Why did they leave?"

"Some say it was malaria, some believe it was a Saracen assault. That's the Temple of Hera on the right. On the left is the Temple of Ceres, goddess of agriculture. Are you up to walking in for a closer view?"

"Most definitely."

Her ankle had barely given her a twinge all day, but she was more than willing to tuck her arm in Marco's for the short stroll to the temples. Her fingers curled into the sleeve of his jacket. She was developing a real attachment to this soft suede. A cold breeze came in off the sea, bringing with it wispy fingers of fog and making her glad she'd worn a black cashmere sweater under *her* jacket.

She spotted only two other visitors in the distance, wandering among the ruins of a small amphitheater. With a little thrill, she saw that she and Marco had the temples to themselves. They approached slowly and mounted the steps at the entrance. Their footsteps echoed on the marble floor. Standing amid columns that had tumbled and been rebuilt gave her the eerie sensation of being part of man's unceasing battle against time and the forces of nature.

"I can almost see a procession of white-robed priests and priestesses," she murmured. "They must have made offerings to Poseidon in hopes he would fill their nets with fish…then wondered how the heck they'd offended him when a storm blew up and sank their ships."

"Something I've wondered, too."

Stricken, she glanced up the man beside her. "Oh, Marco, I'm sorry. I didn't mean to evoke unhappy memories."

"You don't need to apologize." His gaze drifted around the ring of inner columns. "The people who worshipped here thousands of years ago recognized the capriciousness of the gods. That's as good an explanation for Gianetta's drowning as any I've been able to come up with."

The quiet comment mirrored Sabrina's thoughts of a few moments ago. Somehow, putting his wife's death in such a timeless historical context made it a little more understandable. But only a little.

When they exited the temple, Sabrina hugged his arm tight against her side.

"Shall we sit for a moment?" he asked, steering her toward a stone bench strategically positioned for contemplation of the decorative frieze. "I want to follow up on our conversation this morning."

"Which one?" A mischievous smile tugged at her lips. "The one where you told me to open up and say ah? Or the one where we discussed making you my personal physician?"

"The possibility isn't as remote as it sounds. I think you should consider my suggestion of setting up a forward operating location in Rome."

Surprised, she twisted around to face him. "Are you serious?"

"Very much so. Think of the cost savings if you and your partners didn't have to fly back and forth from the States to survey locales or provide an on-site presence for your clients."

The calm reply left Sabrina scrambling for breath. She'd thought they were just indulging in postcoital banter this morning. She had no idea he considered the forward location a viable possibility.

"Caroline and Devon and I just started European Business Services six months ago," she explained. "We don't have the contracts or the resources yet to open an office in Rome."

"I could help. I have a great many connections within the medical community. I also belong to a number of professional associations. Each of these associations rotates their annual conference to various countries."

Her brow creased. "You're offering to steer business my way?"

"If it will keep you in Italy, yes." He held up a palm to forestall her instinctive protest. "I know, I know. You're determined to make a success of EBS on your own. You also don't want me meddling in your negotiations. But entrepreneurs exploit their personal and professional contacts all the time. You're shooting yourself in the foot by not taking advantage of my connections, my so lovely, so enchanting Sabrina."

She couldn't argue with that. EBS had landed their first really big contract because one of men she'd dated in her wilder years had referred his old college buddy. The fact that his buddy just happened to be Cal Logan, CEO of Logan Aerospace, had made for a nice chunk of change.

She wasn't sure why she kept resisting the idea of using Marco's influence. At first, she'd worried his title and obvious wealth would affect her negotiations with the hotel managers she'd come to meet with. Now…

Now she worried her hunger for this man might well be clouding her judgment. All he had to do was toss out the idea of setting up an office in Rome and she was ready to sign a lease!

The thought of staying close to him, of letting this undeniable attraction sizzle into something even hotter, made her heart skip a few beats. Then her gaze shifted to the temple looming just over his shoulder.

Their brief conversation about his dead wife leaped into her head. So did an almost photographic image of the portrait the duchess had shown her.

Gianetta, the beautiful. Gianetta, the tragic. Gianetta, Marco's lost love.

He swore the resemblance was only skin deep. His mother seemed to think otherwise. At this moment, Sabrina didn't know who was closer to the truth.

As if sensing that he'd thrown her a curve ball, Marco lifted her hand and brushed a kiss across her knuckles. "I'm not asking you to decide right this moment. We have until the fourth of January together. Use the days ahead to think about my proposal, yes?"

Right. Uh-huh. Sure.

Like she was going to think of anything else?

Nine

The next morning they kicked off their New Year's Eve celebrations with a slow, delicious session between the sheets.

Sabrina couldn't think of *any* better way to end the old year and get ready to ring in the new—until she joined Marco on the terrace for breakfast. Signora Bertaldi's cappuccino and fresh-baked brioche had her salivating even before she greeted the older woman.

"*Buon mattina,* signora."

"*Buon mattina.*" Beaming, Marco's housekeeper placed a foam-topped porcelain cup before Sabrina. "I don't cook the lentils and sausage this morning because you will eat them tonight, at Palazzo d'Calvetti, yes?"

"I, uh, think so."

Sabrina looked to Marco for guidance. His nod confirmed lentils and sausage were on the menu.

"You must be sure to have both," the cook instructed. "For luck."

"I will."

When she went into the kitchen for the plates she'd kept warming in the oven, Sabrina turned to Marco.

"What's the schedule of events for this evening?"

He leaned back in his chair, looking good enough to eat in tan slacks, a sky-blue oxford shirt with the cuffs rolled up and a white sweater knotted loosely over his shoulders.

"Plan on a long night. Dinner at seven, with thirty or so close family and friends. The ball begins at ten."

"How many attend that?"

"The guest list usually runs to about four hundred. At midnight, we'll watch the fireworks displays from the terrace, with more music and dancing to follow. Those with enough staying power usually try to greet the dawn. But don't feel you have to stay up all night. Your ankle gives us a built-in excuse to go upstairs any time we wish."

"Upstairs?"

"I usually remain in town over Fiesta di San Silvestro and Il Capodanno. It's easier than fighting the crowds jamming the streets. I was going to tell you this morning to pack a few overnight things."

Sabrina wasn't so sure about this sleepover. She could handle a dinner for thirty or so and easily get lost in the crowd of four hundred at the ball, but the prospect of facing the duchess across a breakfast table didn't exactly light her jets.

"Are you sure I won't be intruding on your mother's hospitality?"

"Not at all. I have my own apartments in a separate wing of the palazzo."

That issue resolved, Sabrina addressed a more pressing one.

"We'll have to drive into Naples early enough for me to hit the shops. I need a gown for tonight."

"And some red underwear," he reminded her with a grin that sent little shivers down her back.

Oh, boy! Less than a half hour out of Marco's bed and she wanted back in it. She had it bad, Sabrina realized. *Reeeally* bad.

"And some red underwear," she confirmed with a catch in her breath.

"You might find something to suit you in Positano. A friend of mine owns a boutique that caters to the guests at La Sirenuse."

La Sirenuse, Sabrina recalled, was the five-star hotel with rooms booked a year in advance by movie stars and oil tycoons. If the boutique was good enough for them, it was certainly good enough for her.

"It's worth a shot."

"I'll call Lucia and tell her we'll stop by on our way to Naples. If you don't find something there, I know several good shops in the city."

Two minutes after walking through the front door of Lucia Salvatore's elegant boutique Sabrina knew she'd struck gold. Forewarned by Marco's call, the vivacious owner had three fabulous gowns ready for Sabrina to try on.

She swept out of the dressing area to model each gown for Marco. He heartily approved of the strapless black taffeta with a full skirt that rustled when she walked. He was even more enthusiastic over the shimmering emerald satin that hugged her breasts and waist before exploding into rainbow-colored layers of chiffon. But the gold lamé body sheath won his vote, hands down.

The slinky fabric clung to Sabrina's every curve, shooting off pinpoints of light with each step. The diagonally cut bodice narrowed to a slender strap and was clasped with a jeweled leopard that draped over her left shoulder. The skirt was slit to the thigh on the right side.

"That one," Marco pronounced. "It must be that one."

Sabrina had to agree, especially when Lucia produced a pair of gold sandals with manageable heels.

"Don Marco said you have hurt your ankle and

must take care how you walk. It's good that you are so tall. These should work well for you."

The thong sandals worked very well. Sabrina took a practice turn around the dressing area and didn't wobble once.

"You will need long gloves," Lucia announced. "And for your hair..." She tapped a finger against her lower lip and surveyed her customer with a connoisseur's eye. "You will wear it up to show off our little pet, yes?"

Sabrina swept up her hair with both arms and angled around until the glittering leopard draped over her shoulder caught the light.

"Oh, yes," she murmured to the jeweled beast. "We have to show you off."

"I have just what you need." The boutique owner unlocked a glass case and slid out a hair comb. "It is antique and perhaps a little expensive, but the golden topaz stones are perfect with this dress."

A glimpse at the price tag indicated it was more than a *little* expensive. But Sabrina knew she had to have it the moment she twisted her heavy mane atop her head and anchored it with the comb.

"I'll take it. Now please tell me you have some red briefs in stock."

"Briefs?"

"Briefs, bikinis, hipsters...I'll take whatever you have as long as they're red."

"But do you not wish for ecru with this dress? Or

perhaps…" She stopped, laughing as the light dawned. "Ah, yes. You must wear red for luck."

"That's what I've been told."

"Come with me."

Moments later, the gown went into a zippered bag. Shoes, long gloves, comb and flame-red hipsters went into a tissue-lined tote. Pleased with her purchases, Sabrina dug out her American Express card.

"Oh, no, Ms. Russo."

"You don't take American Express? No problem. We can put it on Visa."

"No, no." The brunette flashed a quick look at the man waiting patiently in the front room of the boutique. "When Don Marco called, I assumed… That is, he told me…"

"Told you what?"

"He said you were his guest and instructed me to send the bill for whatever you purchased to his villa."

Sabrina stiffened, but kept her smile firmly in place. "He's a real sweetie pie, isn't he? Just go ahead and charge the items to my card."

The shop owner looked taken aback at hearing His Excellency referred to as a sweetie pie, but she ran the AmEx card without further discussion. Sabrina signed the ticket and sailed out with her purchases in hand.

"All set."

"Good. Let me take those."

She waited until they were in the Ferrari and on the narrow, winding road out of town to let loose with both barrels.

"Lucia said you told her to send the bills for my purchases to the villa. Do *not* embarrass me like that again."

"Embarrass you?" He looked honestly bewildered. "How does that embarrass you?"

"Oh, come on! Why don't you just take out a billboard ad saying we're lovers?"

His brows snapped together. "I wasn't aware you wanted to disguise the fact."

"I don't! But neither do I want you to pay for my underwear."

With a muttered curse, he pulled the Ferrari into a turnout. Ironically, it was the same turnout where Sabrina had left her rental car to snap pictures of the picturesque town spilling down the cliffs to the sea.

The car halted with a jerk, its nose pointed toward the restless sea. Marco shoved the gearshift into park, set the emergency brake and twisted the key in the ignition before slewing around in his seat. Anger blazed from his eyes.

"I'm not allowed to buy you a gift?"

"A ceramic bowl is a gift. A bottle of perfume is a gift. Two thousand dollars worth of clothing and lingerie crosses the line."

"Who set these rules?" he demanded, his accent thickening with his anger. "One hundred dollars for perfume, *si*. Two thousand dollars for clothing, no."

Thoroughly irritated, Sabrina fell back on the only argument she could. "There are no set rules. Just logic and common sense."

"This may sound logical to you," he retorted. "It doesn't to me."

She scrubbed her forehead with the heel of her hand, hating this argument, hating the memories it brought back of all the times she'd locked horns with her father in an effort to assert her independence, financially and otherwise.

"It's... It's not so much the amount that matters as the way you handled it. You should have consulted me before making an arbitrary decision to foot the bill."

"I ask again. I need to be clear on this, you understand. You want me to consult with you before I buy you any gift, large or small?"

"Yes. No."

He lifted one brow sardonically, and Sabrina gave a frustrated huff.

"Oh, hell, now I don't know what I want."

Her obvious frustration took the edge from Marco's anger. With a visible effort, he reined in his temper.

"We're new to each other," he said in a more even tone. "Still learning this intricate dance. Two steps forward, one back, like a waltz. We're bound to miss a step or two until we perfect our rhythm."

He let his glance shift to the sea. The churning waves held his gaze for long moments. When he turned to her again, all trace of anger was gone.

"I loved one woman and lost her. I don't know yet where we will go, you and I. Neither of us can know at this point. But I *do* know one thing with absolute certainty. I don't want to lose you, Sabrina *mia*."

Now that was hitting below the belt! She could go nose to nose with her father any day, matching his hardheaded stubbornness with her own. Marco's quiet declaration took every ounce of fight out of her. Worse, the tender endearment he attached to her namc turned her insides to mush.

"I don't want to lose you, either."

He framed her face with his palms. "One step forward, my darling."

It was easy, so easy, to take that step. Sighing, she tipped her chin for his kiss.

She had no idea how long they might have sat there, practicing their steps, if a tour bus hadn't pulled into the turnout. The tourists piled out, oohing and ahhing over the incredible view. Their cameras were already clicking when Marco keyed the ignition.

They stopped for a late lunch in Torre Annunziata, a small town in the shadow of brooding Mt. Vesuvius, then had to battle horrendous traffic in Naples. Every other street, it seemed, was blocked in preparation for the night's festivities.

They finally pulled up at Palazzo d'Calvetti a little after five. The butler greeted Marco with the same warmth he'd showed on their previous visit. Bowing to Sabrina, he informed the duke that his mother and sister were in the upstairs salon.

"*Grazie,* Phillippo. Our bags are in the car. Will you have them taken to my apartments?"

"Of course, Your Excellency."

Marco took Sabrina's elbow to help her up the broad staircase and escorted her to a sitting room rich with antiques and bright sunlight. Donna Maria was seated at a gilt trimmed desk with reading glasses perched on the end of her nose, skimming what Sabrina guessed was a last-minute to-do list.

She looked up at their entrance. Pleasure flooded her face at the sight of her son. "Marco! I was beginning to think you would not arrive in time for dinner."

He bent to kiss her on both cheeks. "Traffic was a nightmare, Mama."

The duchess welcomed Sabrina with a voice that was a few degrees warmer than on her previous visit but stopped well short of gushing.

Marco's sister, on the other hand, more than made up her mother's reserve. She was a slender brunette in orange-striped leggings and an eye-popping electric-blue tunic that echoed the blue streak in her short, spiky black hair. With a yelp of delight, she threw herself into her brother's arms for an exuberant reunion.

Laughing, Marco had to cut into her torrent of Italian. "AnnaMaria, be still long enough for me to introduce to my houseguest."

"So this is your American, eh?" She turned in the circle of his arms and raked Sabrina from head to foot with the critical eye of an artist. "Mama told me you look much like Gia. I think... The hair, yes.

The eyes, a little. But not the mouth. Or the bones. Those wonderful bones are yours."

Sabrina could have kissed her!

"Ah, here is Etienne and my beautiful bambinos. Come meet Marco's American."

The burly French sculptor carried a doe-eyed little girl in one arm. A boy of four or five swung like a mischievous chimp from the other. The boy let go only long enough for his father to engulf Sabrina's hand in a thorny palm.

"A pleasure to meet you, Ms. Russo."

"And I, you. I attended an exhibit of your work at New York's Metropolitan Museum of Art a few years ago."

"Ah, *oui.* The Paris au Printemps Exhibition."

He didn't ask her opinion of his work but the question came through in a quizzically raised brow. Sabrina responded with a warm smile.

"I was especially intrigued by one piece. I think it was titled *An Afternoon in Montmartre.* I was amazed at how you captured the quarter's vibrancy in two pieces of twisted metal and a rope of flickering neon."

"AnnaMaria! Take charge of these monkeys! I want to go out on the terrace and speak more with this so very intelligent and charming woman."

"You have no time for flirting, Etienne. If Mama is done with me, we need to feed and bathe the children before we dress for dinner."

"An entire house full of servants," the sculptor

complained with a good-natured grin, "and she insists we feed, scrub and tuck these two in ourselves."

"Go!" the duchess instructed her daughter and son-in-law. "See to your children."

"What can we do to help?" Marco asked his mother.

"Nothing. Everything is as well ordered as it's going to be. But I hope you and Sabrina will excuse me if I, too, go rest a bit before dinner."

"We'll go up, as well. We can unpack and have an aperitif before the hoards arrive."

He and Sabrina accompanied the duchess up the grand staircase and parted company on the third floor.

"You'd best be downstairs by a quarter to seven to greet our guests," she told her son.

"We will."

She turned toward the east wing, hesitated. Her glance flicked from her son to Sabrina and back again. "Have you warned her about the paparazzi?"

"Not yet."

"They could be…difficult."

"We'll don our armor before we come downstairs."

"Bene."

Sabrina contained her curiosity until Marco escorted her into his suite of rooms in the east wing. She caught a glimpse of their bags set side by side on a padded bench in a cavernous bedroom before demanding an explanation.

"What was that about?"

"You're not the only one who has fed the beasts,"

he commented with a dry reference to the articles his mother had pulled off the Internet about her. "They attacked like sharks after Gianetta's death. One tabloid even hinted I had somehow sabotaged the sailboat."

"Dear God! Why would you do that?"

"The usual reasons. Jealousy, anger, to rid myself of an inconvenient wife so I could marry my mistress."

Shrugging, he opened the doors of a parquetry chest to display a well-stocked bar.

"It didn't seem to matter that I *had* no mistress. What would you like to drink?"

"It's going to be a long night. I'd better stick with something nonalcoholic for now."

Marco chinked ice into two glasses and twisted off the lid on a bottle of Chinotto. The dark liquid fizzed like a carbonated drink and had a unique taste that combined bitter and sweet at the same time.

"We always allow a few members of press to take photographs at the ball. Be warned, they'll have an avid interest in you."

"Because I resemble Gianetta?"

His dark eyes held hers. "Because you will be the first woman I've invited to the ball *since* Gianetta."

Ohh-kaay.

Sabrina took another sip of the fizzing soft drink and willed her heart to stop hammering against her ribs. The waltz Marco had described so beautifully earlier suddenly seemed to have picked up in tempo. She couldn't shake the feeling she'd just been swept into a sultry tango.

The tempo kicked up yet again a little over an hour later.

Gowned, gloved, her hair anchored high on her head with the topaz-studded comb, she swept out of the bedroom in a glitter of gold. Two paces into the sitting room she caught sight of Marco and stopped dead.

Her jaw sagged. Her breath got stuck somewhere in the middle of her throat. The best she could manage was a breathless whisper.

"Wow."

"My sentiments exactly," he answered in a low growl. "You look magnificent, Sabrina *mia*."

His eyes devoured her as he crossed the room. Hers drank in the snowy white tie and pleated shirt, the black tails, the jeweled insignia of some royal order pinned to the red sash that slashed across his chest.

Tonight, Sabrina realized as her heart drummed out a wild beat, her handsome doc was every inch a duke.

Ten

Marco wasn't the only one rigged out in royal splendor for the night's festivities.

His mother was stunning in a gown of white satin and a diamond tiara studded with emeralds the size of pigeon eggs. More emeralds cascaded from her ears and throat.

His sister and brother-in-law somehow managed to look both dignified and unconventional, Anna-Maria in a shimmering cobalt gown that highlighted the blue streak in her hair, Etienne in a black cut-away and a jaunty white silk scarf looped over one shoulder in place of a tie.

With everyone dressed so formally, Sabrina expected dinner to be a stiff affair. Instead, the guests were lively and the meal a gastronomical delight that included the expected lentils and savory stuffed sausage.

"For richness of life in the coming year," the retired admiral seated next to Sabrina informed her as he speared a piece of sausage.

She'd already discovered he was Marco's great uncle on his mother's side and a real character. He wore his navy uniform, with thick gold ropes at both shoulders and a chest covered with medals. Bushy white whiskers sprouted from his cheeks and an eye patch covered one eye. His other eye kept trying to get a good look down the front of Sabrina's gown.

Like when he shooed away the hovering waiter and insisted on refilling her wine glass himself.

"Allow me, Signorina."

She rewarded his determined efforts by hunching her shoulders to display a teeeeeny bit more cleavage.

"Ahh," the admiral murmured, his whiskers twitching. *"Bellisima."*

She glanced up in time to catch Marco observing the byplay. Grinning, he lifted his goblet in a silent toast. She responded with a wink.

The mischievous wink hit Marco with almost the same impact as the sight of Sabrina in glowing candlelight. His fingers tightened on the stem of his goblet as he drank in the sight of her.

Until this moment, he'd wanted her with a hunger that seemed to multiply with each passing hour.

Seeing her now, her face framed by those loose, careless tendrils, her eyes alight with laughter, turned hunger into something deeper, something richer. Something that made his heart constrict.

Marco hadn't missed the startled glances Sabrina had drawn when the dinner crowd had first assembled. Most of them had known Gianetta, some well enough to have experienced her wild, almost frenetic highs on occasions like this. But Sabrina's ready smile and genuineness had soon charmed them out of their initial uncertainty.

Nor did she falter during the long, lively banquet. Despite Uncle Pietro's ogling and the fact that most of the conversation was in Italian, she held her own easily with young and old. Not surprising given her privileged background, Marco supposed. As Dominic Russo's only child, she'd no doubt attended many functions like this. Yet Marco felt himself falling a little more in love each time she responded to a question with her less than idiomatic Italian or flashed him a laughing glance.

When her guests had finished their brandy-flamed lemon gateau and after-dinner coffee, the duchess nodded to her son. Marco rose with her.

"We have a half hour before the guests will begin to arrive for the ball," Donna Maria announced. "Please use the time to refresh yourselves or enjoy drinks in the main salon while we do our duty downstairs."

Marco used the loud scrape of chairs and general exodus to explain the drill to Sabrina.

"Mother traditionally grants interviews to society editors and entertainment TV reporters before the ball. It's a good opportunity for her to push her favorite charities and latest projects. Unfortunately, it's become a command performance for Anna-Maria and me, as well. Will you be all right if I desert you for a half hour?"

"I'll be fine." Her eyes twinkled. "Your uncle has offered to show me the gardens by moonlight."

"The old goat!" Curling a knuckle, he brushed it over her cheek. "If I were you, I'd stick to the lighted paths."

"I will," she promised, laughing.

Her rippling amusement stayed with Marco as he joined Etienne to escort the duchess and AnnaMaria down the grand staircase. He couldn't remember the last time he'd taken such delight in the sound of a woman's laugh. Or such intense pleasure from the simple act of touching her.

The aftershocks from that touch were still with him when his mother and AnnaMaria seated themselves on a stiff-backed sofa in the green salon. Marco and Etienne took up places behind them.

Donna Maria's ever efficient secretary had furnished a copy of the guest list to the various papers and TV networks weeks ago. They in turn had submitted their requests for interviews with particular celebrities, which had been coordinated with the individuals involved. Those interviews would be conducted when the guests arrived for the ball. This session focused strictly on the family whose roots went so deep into Neapolitan society.

Donna Maria presented brief prepared remarks before graciously inviting questions. Most concerned the drive she'd just launched on behalf of the victims of the floods that had devastated the village of Camposta. AnnaMaria and Etienne were asked about their latest exhibits. Marco fielded several questions concerning the seventeen-hour surgery he'd performed last month to separate twins conjoined at the base of their skulls.

He was beginning to believe they'd escape the session relatively unscathed with a reporter at the back of the room raised her hand.

"Sophia Ricci here. I have a question for His Excellency, Don Marco."

"Yes?"

The reporter edged to the front of the gathering. She was in her early thirties, with a thin, attractive face and black hair razored into uneven lengths.

"I see a name has been added to the guest list. Ms. Sabrina Russo, of Arlington, Virginia."

When she paused and let a small silence spin out, Marco lifted a brow. "Is that your question?"

"No, Your Excellency. I would like to know if Ms. Russo is the woman you were spotted with yesterday, disembarking from the ferry in Sorrento?"

A stir of palpable interest flowed through the reporters, and Marco smothered a curse. The hounds had picked up the scent sooner than he'd expected.

"She is," he replied.

Pens clicked. Notebook pages flipped. While her rivals scribbled furiously, Ricci's eyes gleamed with the triumph of having scooped them all.

"The same woman my sources tell me is currently staying at your villa?" she asked slyly.

He'd learned long ago the futility of attempting to deny the facts. "That's correct."

"May I ask how you met?"

"Quite by accident. Ms. Russo fell and sprained her ankle. Luckily, I was close by and was able to treat the injury. She's been recuperating at my villa."

"So is she your patient?" Ricci asked with dogged persistence. "Or your lover?"

Donna Maria's head snapped up. AnnaMaria let out a little hiss. Marco forestalled their instinctive responses and answered with the authority bred into him by his heritage and his demanding profession.

"Ms. Russo is my *guest,*" he said coldly. "Now you must excuse us. We've kept her and our other guests waiting long enough."

Ricci was no more immune to his icy stare than first-year residents at the hospital. She stepped back, momentarily cowed, as Marco offered the duchess his arm. Etienne did the same for AnnaMaria.

"That woman will be at her desk all night," Donna Maria predicted grimly as they mounted the grand staircase. "You'd best warn Sabrina to expect the worst."

"I will."

"You know how they flayed Gianetta."

His jaw set. "I know."

How could he not? He'd had to force his way through them, protecting his shuddering, sobbing wife with his body the last time she checked into a rehab clinic.

"Sabrina is stronger than Gia. And…"

He searched for the right word to describe her.

"…and truer to herself," he finished slowly. "She'd have to be, to resist Dominic Russo's attempts to break her."

The duchess halted halfway up the stairs. Marco met her frowning gaze with a steady one of his own. After a long moment his mother blew out a long breath.

"So it's that way, is it?"

"It is for me."

"And for her?"

The tension knotting the cords in his neck eased. "I'm working on that," he said with a wry smile.

The duchess tapped the toe of her jeweled shoe. "You'd better ask her to stand beside you in the receiving line. That might spike the worst of their guns."

Two steps down, AnnaMaria's eyes widened. "Mama! You wouldn't let Etienne stand with us to greet the guests until he made a respectable woman of me."

Her loving husband snorted. "And whose fault was that? You wouldn't agree to marry me until you were well into your ninth month. Have you forgotten how your water broke at the altar?"

"Please!" A pained expression crossed the duchess's face. "Do not remind us. Marco, go find Sabrina."

He located her in a circle that included three of his cousins and a long-time friend of his sister.

The all-female group was hunched forward in their chairs and deep in a discussion of last year's American presidential elections. Not surprisingly, Sabrina heartily agreed with her European counterparts that a woman was more than capable of leading either the U.S. *or* Italy.

"I'm sorry but I need to steal you away," he said with a smile.

She excused herself from her new friends and rose. The long column of her gown shimmered like molten gold as she hooked her arm through his.

"How's your ankle?" Marco asked.

"Good. Except for a *very* short stroll with Uncle Pietro, I've kept off it."

"Can you take a little extra duty? The ball guests are about to arrive. I'd like you to join me in the receiving line."

She slanted him a surprised glance. "You told me this is the first time you've brought a woman to the ball since your wife died. Won't it add fuel to the speculative fire if I'm included in the receiving line?"

"Unfortunately, the fire has already been fueled. One of the reporters downstairs asked about the woman I was spotted with in Sorrento yesterday. She found out you're staying at my villa and wanted to know if we're lovers."

"She asked you that? In front of your mother?"

"She did."

"How did you respond?"

"I told her you were my guest. We left it at that."

Lips pursed, she shook her head. "I seriously doubt it will stay left."

"Probably not. As you Americans say, however, the best offense is a good defense. Or is it the other way around?"

"Beats me."

"No matter. We'll put ourselves in plain sight and let everyone think what they will."

She wasn't convinced. "Don't you think you should clear this with the duchess first?"

"It was her suggestion."

"You're *kidding!*"

He had to smile at her thunderstruck expression. "No, Sabrina *mia,* I am not."

"Well, in that case…" Squaring her shoulders, she pasted on a brilliant smile. "Lead on, McDuff."

Sabrina knew darn well her presence in the receiving line would generate all kinds of speculation.

Sure enough, the guests who streamed into the grand ballroom regarded her with expressions that ranged from mild interest to avid curiosity.

Marco introduced her simply as his guest from America, in Italy on business. But the possessive hand he kept at the small of her back didn't go unnoticed. Nor did the private smiles he gave her between introductions.

Once most of the guests had been received, Marco officially opened the festivities by leading his mother out for the first waltz. Head high, her emerald-and-diamond tiara sparkling in the light, Donna Maria moved with regal grace in her son's arms.

Her next partner was one of the guests of honor—the mayor of the city of Naples—leaving Marco free to cross the parquet floor and hold out a gloved hand to Sabrina.

"Shall we?"

Either by luck or by design, the song was a slow, dreamy Italian love song. Marco held her close. Too close for ballroom protocol, judging by the glimpses Sabrina caught of raised eyebrows. She knew darn well the tight arm around her waist was intended to take most of the strain off her ankle. That didn't stop her from reveling in its hard, muscled strength or delighting in the brush of Marco's lips at her temple.

He was too well mannered to dance only with Sabrina, and far too solicitous of her injury. But before doing his duty with his mother's other guests, he made sure she was comfortably seated in one of the chairs lining the long ballroom. An assortment of his friends and acquaintances were detailed to keep her entertained.

The group included a wiry professional soccer player, who swore he owed the hump in the bridge of his nose from a kick Marco delivered when they were boys, and a sixtyish socialite arrayed in diamonds who regaled them all with stories from her days as stripper. She had everyone in the group helpless with laughter when a young couple caught Sabrina's eye. They stood at the edge of the gathering, hesitant to intrude, until she smiled an invitation.

"Please," she urged. "Join us."

"No, no, Signorina." Keeping an arm curled around his wife's shoulders, the young man demurred. "We come only to wish you happy on this Feast of San Silvestro."

"Thank you. The same to you."

"We see you with His Excellency," his wife said shyly. "We want to tell you… We want you to know…"

She stumbled to a halt and her brown eyes flooded with tears. Concerned, Sabrina started to push to her feet. The young husband stopped her with a quick explanation.

"His Excellency, he operates when no other surgeon would and saves our baby. Theresa and I… We would like to tell you he is a good doctor, a good man."

"I know," Sabrina replied softly.

When the young husband led his wife away, she swept her glance over the vast, mirrored hall until she spotted Marco. So tall, so distinguished in his white tie and tails. So damned handsome.

Yet she knew what she now felt for the man had little to do with his admittedly spectacular exterior. Sometime in the past week, she'd fallen for the whole package. Doc. Duke. Fast driver. So-so chess player. Inexhaustible, inventive, incredible lover.

With a small sigh, she turned her attention back to his friends.

Marco joined the group for the final hour before midnight. Music and laughter filled the ballroom. Tuxedoed waiters circulated with glasses with sparkling spumante. The minute hand on watches and clocks raced toward twelve.

Suddenly the lights dimmed. At a signal from the duchess, servers threw open the tall French doors leading to the wide terrace.

"Naples puts on the most spectacular fireworks display in all Italy," Marco explained. "We can watch in here, where it's warm, or out on the terrace."

Sabrina had spotted outdoor umbrella heaters during her short excursion with the admiral and didn't hesitate. "The terrace, please."

Glasses in hand, they joined the crowd outside and leaned elbows on the wide balustrade to soak in the incredible view of Naples lit up below. Strung out in a crescent of lights, the city circled the ink-black harbor guarded by the brightly illuminated Angevin fortress.

Judging by the noise that rose in waves, every Neapolitan must have spilled out in the streets. Horns honked. Spoons beat against pots. Raucous shouts and laughter competed with the reverberating bass boom of a rock band.

As if on cue, the noise died down. A hush seemed to settle over the city. Then someone on the terrace started a loud countdown.

"Dieci, nove, otto..."

Other voices joined in the chant.

"Sette, sei, cinque, quattro..."

Marco's arm tightened around Sabrina's waist. She turned a laughing face up to his.

"Tre," she sang out with him. *"Due. Uno!"*

His mouth came down on hers and *not* in a polite, celebration kiss. This was a hungry joining that kicked the New Year off with one hell of a start.

Sabrina was so lost in it, so consumed by it, she barely heard the shrill whistle of a rocket launched high into the sky. Marco ended the kiss just as the night exploded in balls of brilliant red.

He hadn't exaggerated, she decided some twenty minutes later. Naples's pyrotechnic display *had* to be the best in Italy. Synchronized to a compilation of Puccini's most famous arias, it was a joyous symphony of color and light and sound. Sabrina enjoyed every moment of the show.

She enjoyed it even more when Marco steered her to a dim corner of the terrace. Hands clasped around her waist, he lifted her to sit on the balustrade. He stood next to her, at eye level for a change.

Roman candles and starbursts continued to explode overhead. The revelry in the streets below reached fever pitch. Yet they might have been alone in the night.

His face cast in shadows, Marco reached up to tuck a wayward strand behind Sabrina's ear. "Do you remember asking me if Italians make New Year's resolutions?"

"I do. And as I recall, you said that was an all-American tradition."

"I've decided to make one tonight."

She had to smile at his solemn expression. "Want to tell me what it is?"

"It's you, Sabrina *mia*."

As if consumed by the need to touch her, Marco drew his fingertips across her cheek, brushed her lips, cupped her chin.

"I know we agreed to move one step at a time. I know you're still wrestling with the idea of opening an office in Rome. I know I'm pushing when I should be patient. But I've resolved to do whatever I can, whatever I must, to keep you in Italy. And in my heart."

Sheer surprise took her breath away.

"That's… That's some resolution," she managed finally on a shaky laugh. "They usually run more to shedding a few pounds or balancing the checkbook."

"My checkbook is balanced and I don't need to lose weight."

She couldn't argue with that. The body pressing against hers was iron hard.

"And just so you know," he murmured as he bent to brush her mouth with his, "I intend to keep this resolution."

Eleven

The ball officially ended at 2:00 a.m., after which the duchess and most of the older guests said good-night. Fifty or so of the younger set partied until dawn.

Marco played host for the champagne breakfast that greeted *Il Capodanno*—New Year's Day. The lavish spread was served on the terrace with the umbrella heaters glowing to chase away the night chill. As the first gold rays of dawn silhouetted the magnificent cathedral dominating Naples's skyline, corks popped and glasses clinked.

Marco tipped his glass to Sabrina's. "To new beginnings."

"To new beginnings," she echoed, her lungs

squeezing at the picture he made in the slowly gathering light.

He'd yanked on the ends of his tie to undo the bow and popped the top two buttons on his white shirt. The tie dangled loosely below a chin and cheeks showing a faint dark bristle. How the hell did he manage to look so sophisticated and so hot at the same time?

"Thank you for including me in these celebrations," she said with a smile. "I've had a wonderful time."

"Ah, but the best is yet to come."

"There's *more?*"

"I'm hoping there will be *less,*" he countered with a slow grin. "I've yet to see you in—or out of—those lacy red briefs you purchased at the boutique."

Sabrina's incipient weariness vaporized on the spot. "I just might be able to accommodate you there, fella. When can we ditch this crowd?"

Luckily, the party was already beginning to break up. Marco's soccer-player friend led the charge by scraping back his chair.

"Time for our traditional *Il Capodanno* swim in the bay," he announced. "Who's with me?"

He recruited ten hearty souls. Another dozen or so decided to tag along to watch. The remaining guests gathered their belongings and left, as well.

"Thank God," Marco muttered when he'd bid the last of them goodbye.

He took the time to thank the servers waiting to

clean up and pass each a generous tip before he turned to Sabrina, his eyes hot.

"I've been waiting for this all night."

The servers exchanged amused smirks as His Excellency scooped her into his arms. More than a little breathless with anticipation, she looped her arms around his neck. Her pulse leaped into high gear as he carried her up the stairs and down the long hall to his private apartments.

Marco kicked the door shut behind them, bent to flip the lock and strode into the master bedroom.

"Now, my beautiful Sabrina, we'll start the New Year in proper style."

He shifted his hold and let her slide slowly, sensuously to her feet. When he reached behind her to remove the topaz-studded comb and let her hair fall free, she felt him against every tingling inch of her. His chest flattened her breasts. His thighs cradled hers. His erection prodded urgently against her belly.

Too hungry for subtleties, Sabrina wedged her hand between their bodies and palmed his rock-hard length. The growl that ripped from the back of his throat shot thrills through her entire body.

He fumbled with the clasp of her gown and gave a frustrated oath when he couldn't figure out how to unhook the glittering leopard draped over her shoulder.

"Here." On fire with need, she brushed aside his hands. "Let me."

The gold lamé slithered over her hips and pooled around her jeweled sandals. Sabrina stepped out of the gown, kicked off her sandals and stood before him, naked except for the red lace hipsters.

"Now you. I want to see you."

He tugged off his tie, tossed it aside and shrugged out of the black tails. The tailored jacket hit the floor. The red sash came off over his head.

Sabrina held on to the sash while he shucked the rest of his clothing. With a wicked smile, she draped the wide red satin over his bare chest.

"There. Now we're a matched set."

She realized her mistake the moment he tumbled her to the bed and the jeweled decoration pin gouged into her left breast.

"Oooops! That's gotta go."

She wiggled out from under him and yanked the sash over his head again. Marco used the brief separation to tug down her panties. Kneeing her legs apart, he repositioned himself between her thighs and surged into her with an urgency that had Sabrina gasping with delight.

It must have been the long night. Maybe the champagne. Whatever the reason, it didn't occur to her that they hadn't so much as *thought* about a condom until he pulled out and thrust in again. By then, she was beyond stopping him *or* herself.

Marco dragged himself out of bed before noon but insisted Sabrina burrow in to catch up on missed sleep. She didn't argue. The long night and early morning activities had drained her.

She woke again around 3:00 p.m. and stretched languorously before padding into the bathroom. A hot, pounding shower sluiced away the lingering effects of the long night and the aftermath of their lovemaking. In the midst of soaping off the sticky residue between her thighs, she had to battle a sudden wave of worry.

Okay. All right. No need to panic. One bout of glorious, reckless sex did not a baby make. Hopefully!

Unless…

Her fingers clenched on the washcloth as Marco's New Year resolution leaped into her head. How had he phrased it? He would do whatever he could, whatever he had to, to keep her in Italy.

She dismissed the nasty suspicion almost as soon as it surfaced. No way he would stoop to that kind of dirty trick. Besides, even if one of his sperm *had* snuggled in, it would be weeks before the wiggly little tadpole made its presence known. Much too late to influence her decision to stay or not stay in Italy.

"C'mon, girl," she admonished as she rinsed off the soapy suds. "You need to get a grip *and* get your butt in gear."

Not sure of the plans for the rest of the day, she pulled on her calf-length black crinkle skirt and topped it with the fitted velvet jacket. Her ankle didn't give her so much as a twinge when slid on the black-beaded ballet shoes.

Consequently, she had a spring in her step when she exited the east wing and followed the blare of a TV to a sunny reading room overlooking the back terrace.

Marco was there, looking sexy as hell in snug jeans and a gray Italian-knit sweater that emphasized his wide shoulders. The duchess, AnnaMaria and Etienne were also present. Each of them had their eyes locked on the flat-screen TV mounted on the far wall. It was showing footage from the ball, Sabrina saw as she pitched her voice to be heard above the announcer.

"Happy New Year."

Four heads whipped in her direction. The duchess shot upright in her chair and waved an imperious hand at her son as she returned the greeting.

"Happy New Year. Marco, please turn off that annoying noise."

"You can leave it on. I'd like to see the…"

She broke off, her jaw sagging as a new image filled the screen.

There she was, in vivid high definition. Stretched out on a beach towel. Nude from the waist up. Her pubic area covered—barely!—by the minuscule triangle of her string bikini. With two small black squares blanking her nipples from the viewing audience.

She caught only a brief glimpse of the background before Marco stabbed the remote and killed the screen. It didn't matter. She knew exactly where and when that picture had been shot: Ipanema Beach—Rio—spring break of her senior year. With dozens of similarly clad coeds soaking up the sun on either side of her.

That was before MySpace and YouTube, so the photo had enjoyed only a brief shelf life in the tabloids. Not brief enough, obviously. The enterprising reporter who'd asked Marco about his new lover must have dug it out of the dustbin.

"Well, that didn't take long," she drawled, as embarrassed as she was chagrined.

"It doesn't matter," Marco replied with a shrug. "Women wear less than that on our beaches."

"True, but TV stations don't intersperse their pictures with footage from your mother's New Year's Eve gala." She blew out a ragged breath and turned to the duchess. "I'm sorry, Donna Maria. Very sorry."

"It's of no account," the older woman said with a shrug. "We have survived worse."

Sabrina couldn't quite hold back a wince.

"She means me," AnnaMaria interjected. "I almost gave birth to my son at the altar. The gossip columns, the cartoons, they ran with it for weeks. And Gia..." She pursed her lips in a moue of disgust. "That one made all our lives hell. Marco, especially, could not..."

"That's enough."

She flashed her brother an annoyed look but

yielded to his quiet command. Sabrina ignored the byplay. Her gaze had snagged on the newspapers scattered across the marble-topped coffee table. One was folded open to what was obviously the society page. A collage of the celebrities who'd attended the ball filled the top half of the page. The bottom half featured Sabrina's picture side by side with that of a vibrant Gianetta in a diamond tiara and an off-the-shoulder gown. The caption below the photos was in big, bold print.

"Sosia della moglie?" Sabrina struggled with the translation. "What does that mean?"

"It's nothing." Marco wadded the paper in his fist. "Nothing."

"Tell me."

With a muttered curse, he tossed the paper in a trash basket. "It translates loosely to 'the wife's counterpart'?"

"Oh. Of course. By counterpart, I suppose they mean double. I should have guessed it was something like that." She lifted her chin and pasted on a brittle smile. "So what are the plans for the rest of the day?"

"Sabrina, all this means nothing."

"If you say so."

He crossed the room in two strides and grasped her upper arms. "Listen to me. It means nothing. The hype, the speculation, it's only to sell papers."

"I know."

"You say that, but your eyes are flat and cold."

The eyes he'd just referred to flashed hot.

"Back off," she warned, her voice low. "This isn't something I want to discuss in front of your family."

"Very well. We'll discuss it privately."

He released her, strode across the room and bent to kiss his mother's cheeks.

"I'm taking Sabrina home, Mama. I'll speak with you soon, yes?"

"See that you do."

"*Ciao,* Etienne. AnnaMaria, kiss those brats of yours for me."

With Marco standing impatiently at the door, Sabrina had no choice but to thank the duchess for her hospitality and apologize once again for the less than flattering publicity.

"It will be old news by five o'clock," the older woman replied with a dismissive wave of her hand.

Right, Sabrina thought as she exchanged kisses with AnnaMaria and Etienne. It would.

Unless she and Marco continued their affair.

Sabrina's stomach churned throughout the drive back to Marco's villa.

Not over the substitute-wife headline. Or the seminude shot. Thank God they'd gone with that instead of the one an enterprising reporter had snapped after she'd stumbled out of party in a Los Angeles watering spot and promptly thrown up on the street.

What made her feel physically ill was the thought of putting Marco and his family through a repeat of what they'd gone through with Gianetta. Sabrina didn't know all the gritty details, but the few she *did* know cast a decided shadow over her romance with the handsome doc.

She couldn't blame anyone but herself for that shadow. She'd been so stubborn, so determined to resist the mold her father kept trying to squeeze her into, that she'd almost made a career of walking on the wild side. Now her past had come back to haunt her with a vengeance.

Miserable, she knew she had to articulate her feelings to Marco. She couldn't do it in the Ferrari, though. Not when its driver had to contend with hairpin turns and the rapidly descending dusk.

By the time they reached the villa, night had shaded the sea outside the windows to midnight blue. The restless waves crashed against the rocks below as Sabrina stood at the window, arms looped around her waist. Marco poured two snifters of brandy, handed her one and tipped his glass to hers.

"All right. We're alone. No sharp curves or oncoming headlights to distract us. Tell me why your eyes went so cold and empty when you looked at me this afternoon."

"It wasn't you. It was that newspaper—the photos—the caption." Her mouth twisted. "The wife's counterpart. God!"

"You don't believe that's why I want you, do you? As a substitute for Gianetta?" His eyes burned into her. "You can't believe it. Not for a minute."

"Of course not! But apparently that's what everyone else believes."

"Everyone, or a handful of editors and television producers who'll push garbage to build their audiences?"

"Oh, c'mon Marco. You saw the looks your friends gave me last night. The curiosity, the speculation they tried so hard to disguise."

"I saw them charmed out of that curiosity by an American beauty who bears only a superficial resemblance to the woman they once knew."

"How can you be so sure it's superficial?" Sabrina fired back. "You don't know me. You don't know my past. Trust me, there's enough juice there to give your handful of editors and television producers multiple orgasms."

"I don't care about your past. What I care about is *our* future."

"So do I!" She took a sip of the fiery brandy for courage and braced her shoulders. "That's why I think I should hop a plane to Barcelona tomorrow. I'll consult with my partner while things cool down here."

"Cool down?" His nostrils flared, as if the phrase had a bad smell. "You're leaving because of a few newspaper articles? I didn't think you were such a coward, Sabrina."

Stung, she lifted her chin. "Not a coward, a realist."

"Then we live with different realities," he snapped.

"Maybe we do!"

Okay, this wasn't how she'd intended the discussion to go. Dragging in a steadying breath, she tried for calm and rational.

"Everything happened so fast between us, Marco. A twisted ankle, a couple of games of chess and we jump into bed with each other. Next thing we know, my boobs are spotlighted on the Italian TV."

He wasn't buying calm *or* rational. Anger simmered in his terse response. "So your solution is to run away?"

"I'm not running away. I've got a bid proposal to finalize. I'll meet my partner in Barcelona, take care of business, and… And…"

"And what?"

He wasn't even *trying* to meet her halfway. Sabrina set her jaw and fought to hold on to her temper. She was doing this for his own good, dammit!

"And I'll call you."

His eyes narrowed. Above the V of his sweater, the cords of his neck stood out.

"You forget my New Year's resolution. Do you think I'll let you just pile into your rental car tomorrow and drive away from me?"

Her breath hissed out. With great care, she set her snifter aside.

"Let?" she echoed.

Impatience stamped across his features. "You know how I mean that."

"No, I don't. But I'm open to an interpretation."

"For God's sake, I'm not going to tie you to the

bed. Although I must admit," he added savagely, "the idea holds great appeal at the moment."

The sheer ridiculousness of that dissolved Sabrina's anger. She bit her lip, trying to hold back a grin, then gave in to her baser self.

"It sounds pretty good to me, too."

Marco's rigid shoulders relaxed. Against his will, against his every instinct, he let her tease him out of his anger. With an exasperated oath, he curled a hand around the nape of her neck and tugged her against him.

"Didn't anyone ever tell you to be careful what you wish for, Sabrina *mia?*"

She was sure he understood her intent. Absolutely convinced he knew she would leave in the morning. Otherwise Sabrina would have never spent those incredibly erotic hours with Italian silk ties knotted around her wrists.

When she emerged from the shower the next morning and told him she intended to call and change her flight yet again, Marco's brows snapped together.

"I thought we settled that."

"We did."

He rolled out of bed and dragged on his jeans in one fluid move. "You can't really want to leave."

"I don't."

Her gaze drifted to the ties still dangling from the bedposts. Everything in her ached for a repeat performance, but with Marco helpless and at *her* mercy this time. Sighing, she pleaded with him to understand.

"We need to give this some time and let the news hounds lock on to another juicy bone."

"Don't include me in that 'we.' I know what I want."

"Okay, *I* need a little time."

His jaw set. "How much time?"

"I don't know."

"A week? A month?"

"I don't know."

"And what am I supposed to do? Sit on my hands and wait until you decide the right time for us?"

The idea he might *not* wait made her feel a little sick but Sabrina didn't back down.

"I guess that's your call, Marco."

His eyes locked with hers for long, tense moments. Then his head dipped in a stiff nod.

"I'll go and make coffee. Buzz me when you're packed. I'll carry your bags upstairs."

Twelve

Sabrina hit the Autostrada and reached Rome's Ciampino Airport in time to turn in her rental car and catch a three-twelve flight to Barcelona.

She zinged Caroline an e-mail as soon as she purchased her ticket. Caro responded immediately, saying she would pick her up at the international terminal.

When she rolled her bag outside the Barcelona terminal, Sabrina was expecting to see her partner wave at her from the driver's side window of a green mini and cut over to the curb. She *wasn't* expecting the auburn-haired female who popped out of the passenger seat.

"Devon! What are you doing here?"

"Cal had to fly home for a few days," the tall, leggy redhead explained, enveloping Sabrina in a fierce hug. "I can't press ahead with the Logan Aerospace/Hauptmann Metal Works integration conference until I get his final list of attendees. So I decided to take a break from all the snow and ice in Austria and zip down to help Caro with the last of her site surveys. Here, let's toss your bag in the trunk and hit the road."

Sabrina climbed into the backseat. Devon got into the front and twisted around, her brown eyes sympathetic. "Caro filled me in on your close encounters of the ducal kind. We're dying to hear what happened."

"Not until we get to the hotel," Caroline pleaded as she struggled to nose the Mini into bumper-to-bumper airport traffic. "I don't want to miss anything. And you guys need to help me navigate."

Luckily the airport was less than ten kilometers from the resort Caro had made her home base. The pastel-hued hotel ringed a free-form pool fringed with rustling palms. Just yards from the sparkling turquoise pool, colorful sailboats and windsurfers cut through the blue-green waters of the Mediterranean.

The lobby reflected the area's rich history in its Moorish arches and bright Catalonian tiles, but the three friends barely took time to glance around before heading right for the elevators.

"I upgraded to a suite when you guys decided to fly in," Caro informed her partners. "At no cost to our client, of course."

Sabrina and Devon exchanged glances. Careful, precise Caroline Walters. They knew they could trust her to always—*always!*—play by the rules. She'd broken them once and paid a vicious price. Ever since, she'd walked the straight and narrow. Sabrina, on the other hand, was still paying for her past.

She waited to share the gory details until they all kicked off their shoes and plopped into chaise lounges on the suite's sun-drenched balcony with glasses of a local Spanish red in hand.

After admitting she'd fallen in lust at first sight, she described her time with the doc before cutting to the disastrous aftermath of the New Year's Eve ball.

"God, you should have seen the TV clip! They led off with shots of guests in long gowns and tuxes, looking so dignified as they mounted the front steps of Palazzo d'Calvetti. Then yours truly fills the screen, wearing nothing but a string bikini bottom and a stupid grin."

"They'd showed all?" Devon asked incredulously.

"All but two digital pasties blacking out my nipples."

"Whew! I can imagine how the duchess reacted. Caro tells me she's a real bitch."

"Actually, she was pretty cool about it."

Sabrina twirled the stem of her wineglass, surprised all over again Donna Maria's attempt to minimize the embarrassing incident.

"She said they'd survived worse."

Sympathy filled Caro's mist-green eyes. Devon just shook her head.

"That had to make you squirm."

"No kidding."

This is what friends were for, Sabrina thought as the tight knot in her stomach loosened a little. This is why the three of them had remained so close since that wild, wonderful year they'd roomed together at the University of Salzburg. She needed to be here with them, needed to talk through the emotions that had piled up on her in the past week.

"Marco's family has endured so much. His grandfather was gunned down on the steps of his home by Naples's version of the mafia. His father died when he was just a child. His wife was lost at sea."

She swirled her wine again, remembering the scene in the library when Marco had stared unseeing out the windows. Remembering, too, the rigid set to his shoulders as he described his wife's tragic drowning.

"He loved Gianetta—really loved her. Her death devastated him. I think he still blames himself for not getting to Naples in time to stop her from taking the boat out. I can't stand the thought of putting him through the emotional wringer again by having my picture splashed up next to his dead wife's all the time."

Devon cocked her head. Her hair spilled over her shoulder, glinting with red-gold highlights in the bright sun as she let loose with the unerring aim of an old friend.

"You don't want to put *him* through that, 'Rina? Or yourself?"

"Hey, you try standing in for a ghost sometime!"

"Do you really think that's what Marco wants? A replacement for his dead wife?"

"He said he doesn't."

"But you don't you believe him?"

"Yes, I believe him."

She did. She really did. From the first night in Marco's arms, she never doubted he was making love to her and not a memory.

"I guess… I guess it all just got to me."

"No surprise there," Caro put in with fierce loyalty. "You've had photographers snapping at your heels for most of your life."

"True," Sabrina admitted wryly. "And I did my damnedest to give them a show."

Devon brushed away the past with an impatient flick of her hand. "Let's talk about now, 'Rina. Inquiring minds want to know. What are you going to do about Marco?"

"Well…"

Her glance shifted to the waves rolling onto the beach below. They foamed on the shore, one after another, with a blessedly soporific effect.

"For the next few days, I'm not going to do anything but sit in the sun and think about his suggestion that we open a satellite office in Rome."

Devon's eyes widened. "He suggested an office in Rome?"

"He did. He also volunteered to use his contacts in the medical community to steer business our way."

Dev looked thoughtful as she turned the possibilities over in her mind. "You know, a liaison here in Europe might not be such a bad idea. It would sure cut down on travel costs."

"And provide a home base when we're working conferences or meetings over here," Caro added. "Definitely something to think about."

"That's exactly what I plan to do." Easing back, Sabrina stretched her legs out on the chaise. "Lay in the sun and think."

"Wrong," Devon countered briskly. "We have a proposal to put together, girlfriend. While Caro and I check out the last few sites, you can sit in the sun and crunch numbers."

Oddly, it was the sun that resolved Sabrina's nagging doubts early the next morning. Or rather, the lack of sun.

Caro and Devon had already left to scout the last two conference sites when thunderclouds rolled in and wind began to lash the palm trees lining the beach. Sabrina braved the elements to take her coffee mug out onto the balcony. She stood there with her hair whipping around her face and watched the sailboats and windsurfers scuttle in to shore.

Lightning arced through the darkening sky. Thunder boomed. Her heart thudded against her ribs. This was the kind of fierce Mediterranean storm that caught Gianetta. This was what killed her.

As if to punctuate her grim thoughts, another tongue of lightning speared down. The blinding flash seemed to sear right through Sabrina's doubts and confusion.

Marco's wife was dead.

Lost forever.

But *she* was alive.

Who knew how long they had? Who knew how long anyone had? Gianetta's tragic death had proved that. Yet here she was, dithering away time they might be spending together.

"Damn!" Sabrina slammed the coffee mug against the balcony rail. "I'm such a friggin' idiot."

Another ominous rumble of thunder sent her racing back into the suite. A frantic call to the airport verified there was a flight leaving for Naples in a little over two hours. A second call went to Devon's cell phone.

"It just occurred to me," she announced breathlessly. "None of us is going to live forever."

"*That* just occurred to you?"

"I could get hit by a car crossing the street. You could choke on a martini olive."

"I don't drink martinis," her bewildered partner countered.

"The point is, none of us know how much time we have left. It could be years. It could be days. Whatever time I've got, I going to spend it with Marco. Every minute. Every second. I want him. I love him."

"Then for God's sake, go get him."

"I'm on my way."

Sabrina slammed down the receiver, swore, and yanked it up again.

"I need a taxi," she informed the front desk.

It took her all of five minutes to change into a pair of jeans, a black, long-sleeved T-shirt and her faithful beaded flats. Another five to throw her things into her roller bag.

An hour and thirty minutes later, her Alitalia flight was skirting the storm that had rolled in off the sea and giving her one hell of a bumpy ride.

The front stretched all the way across the Mediterranean. Sabrina's flight landed at the Naples Airport in a torrential downpour. Soaked to the skin after a dash across the open rental car lot, she threw her bag in the trunk and set out for Marco's seaside villa.

Tackling those narrow, twisting roads in a car with windshield wipers sweeping furiously from side to side was *not* something Sabrina wanted to do again. Ever! She reached the villa a little past 1:00 p.m., dashed through the rain to the covered entry and leaned on the doorbell.

Rafaela's very surprised mama opened the door. "Signorina Russo! His Excellency does not tell me you are coming back."

"He didn't know."

"Come in, come in."

Shaking off water like a golden retriever, Sabrina stepped into the foyer. "Is Don Marco downstairs?"

"No, Signorina. He goes to Roma last night."

"Rome! But I thought… I was sure he told me he didn't have to return to the city until January fifth."

"The hospital calls," Signora Bertaldi explained. "There was an accident. A young boy, I think. His spine is crushed. They operate today."

Sabrina threw a look over her shoulder. Rain still pounded the foyer windows with unrelenting fury. Swallowing a sigh, she turned back to Signora Bertaldi.

"Do you know which hospital he went to?"

"But of course. *Bambino Gesù*. It is the finest children's hospital in Italy."

"Thanks. *Ciao,* Signora."

"Wait! You cannot drive to Roma in such a storm. Stay here until the rain stops."

She might have yielded to the older woman's urging if a thunderous boom hadn't reverberated across the sky at that moment. The storm sounded as if it would settle in the foreseeable future.

"If Don Marco calls," she said with a determined smile, "tell him I'm on my way to Rome."

Gritting her teeth, she tackled the coast roads again. A permanent knot had formed between her shoulder blades by the time she hit the Autostrada.

From that point it should have been an easy two-hour drive into Rome. Instead, the trip took a nerve-grinding four. Italians weren't as obsessed with speed as Germans, but they could lay it on when they wanted to. In a rainstorm like this one, the results often spelled disaster.

One pile-up snarled traffic for at least forty minutes. The second accident was on the other side of the divided highway but rubbernecking drivers in Sabrina's lanes dropped the pace to a near crawl.

Consequently, she hit Rome's sprawling outskirts just in time for the evening rush hour. Most of the commuters were headed out of the city, thank God, but the rain and busy city streets made even going against the bumper-to-bumper flow a nightmare.

She got lost twice trying to find the children's hospital. When she finally pulled into its parking lot, her jaw ached from grinding her teeth. Rain pelted her head and shoulders as she rushed into the lobby. Her soggy ballet shoes squishing, she zeroed in on the reception desk.

"Dr. Calvetti was supposed to operate here today," she said in her halting Italian. "Can you tell me if he's finished with the surgery?"

A few clicks of a keyboard returned the information that Dr. Calvetti was still in Operating Theater 2. Sabrina got directions to the surgical waiting room and hit the elevators.

One glimpse of the couple hunched side by side in the waiting room convinced her she shouldn't intrude. The boy's parents, she guessed. They were in their early thirties, but fear added years to their white, strained faces. Other family members clustered around them, tense and silent.

Sabrina backed away and opted to pace at the end of the hall. She was too antsy to sit after the long drive in any case…and too unsure of what Marco's reaction would be when he saw her.

Her wet, rubber-soled shoes squeaked on the tiles. With each step she breathed in the smell of antiseptic and tried not to remember the uneasy sensation in the pit of her stomach when Marco had asked what he was supposed to do while she took time to think.

She'd left him only yesterday morning. He couldn't have changed his mind about her, about what they could have together, in such a short time.

Except…

She'd changed hers.

With a little groan, Sabrina rubbed the wet sleeves of her T-shirt to disperse the goose bumps. She needed coffee, she decided—hot, steaming coffee. Better yet, the sledgehammer wallop of espresso.

The waiting room probably had a pot going but again she hesitated to intrude. Instead, she searched out a vending machine one floor down. The face that looked back at her from the machine's mirrored front drew another groan.

She looked like a hungover raccoon. Her hair straggled in wet tails. She'd chewed off any trace of lip gloss. Smudged mascara ringed her eyes. Grimacing, she grabbed her espresso and made a quick side trip to the ladies' room to attack the smears with a wet paper towel. A quick comb and a swipe of gloss later, she tossed down the thick, black coffee and headed back upstairs.

The caffeine provided exactly the jolt she needed. Sabrina was still savoring its bite when she reached the surgical waiting area. Loud, wracking sobs from the waiting room stopped her in her tracks.

Dread crashed through her in swamping waves. In her mind's eye, she saw that desperate couple hunched together. Aching for them, Sabrina peered into the waiting room.

The scene inside confirmed her worst fears. Marco was there, wearing green scrubs and antibacterial booties over his shoes. A surgical mask dangled from his neck. He had an arm around the shoulders of a woman who leaned into his chest, weeping uncontrollably.

Sabrina's heart sank like a stone.

It leaped up again a moment later, when the woman tipped her head back.

Those were tears of joy! She was smiling brilliantly through her sobs. And her husband stood beside her, pumping Marco's hand over and over.

"Thank you, Doctor. Thank you. Thank you."

Sabrina couldn't help it. She welled up, too. Big, fat tears that soon had her nose and eyes running like faucets. Edging away from the waiting room, she waited for Marco in the hall.

He emerged a good ten minutes later, smiling and rubbing the back of his neck. He looked both elated and totally exhausted.

Then he saw her.

Slowly, so slowly, he lowered his arm. She waited, her heart hammering, while his glance dropped from her still damp hair to her squishy shoes.

"Why are you wet?"

She gave a shaky laugh. She'd lined up answers to all the questions she'd thought he might ask her. That wasn't one of them.

"It's raining out. Has been all day."

He turned to the windows and lifted a brow in surprise. "So it is."

"How long have you been in surgery?"

"Since ten this morning."

"The boy? He's okay?"

"He'll need months of physical therapy, but I think he'll walk. But how did you know…?"

"I flew into Naples and drove to the villa. Signora Bertaldi told me you were here. So I jumped back in the car and drove to Rome."

"From Positano?" The beginning of a smile tugged at his mouth. "You must have ridden the brake all the way to the Autostrada."

"Pretty much."

"Why, Sabrina? Why are you here?"

At last! The question she'd been waiting for.

"I thought maybe you could help me find an office to lease."

A smile spread across his face, wiping out the lines of exhaustion. He strode over to her and cupped a hand under her chin.

"Before I drag you into the nearest exam room, tell me what brought you back."

"My New Year's resolution."

"I don't remember you making one."

"I did—that day we had dinner with your mother. We were in her Rolls driving through Naples. It hit me that we only had a few more days together. I vowed then and there to make the most of every minute."

"And now?"

"Now we have all the time in the world," she said with a misty smile, "and I intend to make the most of every minute. If you're a good boy, I might even teach you a few new chess moves."

Grinning, he wrapped an arm around her waist. All Sabrina had to do was lean against him to know she'd come home.

"You'll find me a very apt pupil. As long as the game is strip chess."

* * * * *

Silhouette Desire kicks off 2009 with
MAN OF THE MONTH,
a yearlong program featuring
incredible heroes by stellar authors.

When navy SEAL Hunter Cabot returns home for some much-needed R & R, he discovers he's a married man. There's just one problem: he's never met his "bride."

Enjoy this sneak peek at Maureen Child's
AN OFFICER AND A MILLIONAIRE.
Available January 2009 from Silhouette Desire.

One

Hunter Cabot, Navy SEAL, had a healing bullet wound in his side, thirty days' leave and, apparently, a wife he'd never met.

On the drive into his hometown of Springville, California, he stopped for gas at Charlie Evans's service station. That's where the trouble started.

"Hunter! Man, it's good to see you! Margie didn't tell us you were coming home."

"Margie?" Hunter leaned back against the front fender of his black pickup truck and winced as his side gave a small twinge of pain. Silently then, he watched as the man he'd known since high school filled his tank.

Charlie grinned, shook his head and pumped gas.

"Guess your wife was lookin' for a little 'alone' time with you, huh?"

"My—" Hunter couldn't even say the word. *Wife?* He didn't have a wife. "Look, Charlie…"

"Don't blame her, of course," his friend said with a wink as he finished up and put the gas cap back on. "You being gone all the time with the SEALs must be hard on the ol' love life."

He'd never had any complaints, Hunter thought, frowning at the man still talking a mile a minute. "What're you—"

"Bet Margie's anxious to see you. She told us all about that R & R trip you two took to Bali." Charlie's dark brown eyebrows lifted and wiggled.

"Charlie…"

"Hey, it's okay, you don't have to say a thing, man."

What the hell could he say? Hunter shook his head, paid for his gas and as he left, told himself Charlie was just losing it. Maybe the guy had been smelling gas fumes too long.

But as it turned out, it wasn't just Charlie. Stopped at a red light on Main Street, Hunter glanced out his window to smile at Mrs. Harker, his second-grade teacher who was now at least a hundred years old. In the middle of the crosswalk, the old lady stopped and shouted, "Hunter Cabot, you've got yourself a wonderful wife. I hope you appreciate her."

Scowling now, he only nodded at the old woman—the only teacher who'd ever scared the crap out of him. What the hell was going on here? Was everyone but him nuts?

His temper beginning to boil, he put up with a few more comments about his "wife" on the drive through town before finally pulling into the wide, circular drive leading to the Cabot mansion. Hunter didn't have a clue what was going on, but he planned to get to the bottom of it. Fast.

He grabbed his duffel bag, stalked into the house and paid no attention to the housekeeper, who ran at him, fluttering both hands. "Mr. Hunter!"

"Sorry, Sophie," he called out over his shoulder as he took the stairs two at a time. "Need a shower, then we'll talk."

He marched down the long, carpeted hallway to the rooms that were always kept ready for him. In his suite, Hunter tossed the duffel down and stopped dead. The shower in his bathroom was running. His *wife?*

Anger and curiosity boiled in his gut, creating a churning mass that had him moving forward without even thinking about it. He opened the bathroom door to a wall of steam and the sound of a woman singing—off-key. Margie, no doubt.

Well, if she was his wife…Hunter walked across the room, yanked the shower door open and stared in at a curvy, naked, temptingly wet woman.

She whirled to face him, slapping her arms across her naked body while she gave a short, terrified scream.

Hunter smiled. "Hi, honey. I'm home."

* * * * *